A THIN LINE BETWEEN LUST & LOVE

SECRET AFFAIRS

Dedications

I dedicate this body of work to any and everyone who has ever had a dream and thought it was too big to accomplish. As you read this, know that you can and will succeed. How do I know? You are reading mine. Dream big and go harder.

Acknowledgments

First giving all honor and glory to God, I'd like to thank my husband, Bernard for all of his love, support, and patience. To mother, Janice Williams for her loving support. It's not every day that you have an avid reader, who so happens to be a retired Language Arts teacher, at your disposal. So if my subjects and verbs do not agree, or perhaps you come across some misspelled words, blame her. I'm just kidding, but thank you, mommy, for everything. You are priceless. To my dad, Larry Gosha who is my cheerleader. I thank you, dad, for everything as well; your encouragement matters greatly. Thank you to my family and friends for your support as well. As you can see, I can't take full credit for any of this. I am so grateful to those who have come into my life to inspire and motivate me. To you, I say thank you as well.

To the Reader: I thank you for taking out the time to read this novella series. Hang on to your hats, wigs, and everything else in between. **Let the drama begin...**

Chapter 1

BENJAMIN

I have so much on my mind right now. The last place I needed to be was here. Mentally, my mind was across town, but physically, my body was sitting on the first pew of St. Peter's Baptist Church next to my mother, the First Lady. She was glad that I could attend service today and would have been happier had my brother or I followed in the footsteps of our father, the pastor. But my brother and I knew all too well that many were called, and only a few were chosen, and we were neither the chosen nor the called.

Our parents naturally assumed that we would have joined the ministry because that's what Pop had done, and his father before him. Years ago, he approached us about attending seminary school, but we told our parents we wanted a different career path. This, however, didn't go over too well in the beginning. Pop argued that we should follow in his footsteps, regardless.

"Who will take over as pastor after I'm gone if neither one of my own sons won't, or just flat out refuse to? That church has been in our family for more than sixty years. This is the very same church that helped raise your ungrateful behinds, and you two won't even give it a second thought to carry on your father's family tradition. That's just shameful!" Pop said, fussing at us. I later found out this was not so much of us not wanting to become ministers that upset Pop as we did not want to be just like him.

After the choir finished singing their last selection, Pop walked to the podium to introduce his message. He told us to turn our Bibles to 2 Corinthians 5:17. As Pop spoke, his voice faded in the background as my thoughts drifted back to my dilemma. I'm seeing this incredible woman, and my feelings for her have become very strong, but there's also someone else in the picture. I knew I had to cut ties with the other woman, but how?

The how to part was finally coming to me when Pop startled me back into reality. He was standing in front of me, **"Are you a new man, son?!"** He shouted, with his mic in one hand and pointing his index finger at me with the other.

Stunned, all I could do at first was nod my head up and down. "Yes, Sir. I am a new man," I finally replied.

Indeed, I was a new man, but for another reason. This one woman changed my entire outlook on life as I knew it.

"Are you a new man in Christ, church? If so, let the church say amen." Pop said as he closed out his sermon. Amens, hallelujahs, and preach preachers were shouted all over the sanctuary.

I was glad Pop wrapped the service up because I was ready to feed my face. I took my parents to one of our favorite family barbeque spots. Of course, it was jam-packed like any other place on a Sunday afternoon, but we didn't have to wait long.

"Thank you, son, for taking us to dinner. But you know, I'd rather cook," Ma said as we were being seated.

That's my mama always taking care of us. She was the most thoughtful person I knew. "That's okay, Ma. I enjoy spending time with you and Pop."

"What did you get out of today's sermon, son?" He asked, staring me square in the eyes while setting aside his menu.

"A lot. You really had them riled up today, Pop."

"Please, that was the Lord. I'm merely His messenger." He said, correcting me.

"I'm going to download today's service and watch it when I get a chance."

"Un-huh, just what I thought. You weren't paying any attention."

"Greg, you leave my baby alone. He just got home from a business trip. It's a wonder that he made it to church at all."

"Ah, Gloria, I just wanted to know if he received anything from it." He said, getting ready to gripe about her being too overprotective.

I had to jump in before this became World War III. My mama always took up for us. I guess she thought Pop was always riding us, and it wasn't true. He just wanted us to be the men he raised us to be by putting God first and allowing the rest to follow.

"Pop, I promise to watch the sermon from today and all of the others I missed from a couple of weeks ago."

"That's good, son, but let me ask you something that's if mother hen over here don't mind." He said, looking at Ma, who then rolled her eyes at him. He winked at her, trying to make her blush, and it worked. Despite him being who he was, his only weakness was her, and he couldn't stand Ma being mad at him. "Who's this young lady that had your mind today?" Pop caught me off guard again with another question. Ma had even put her fork down and stopped chewing her salad just to hear my response. They knew I rarely brought or mentioned any women to them. They wouldn't prefer the type of women I sometimes kept company with. I stopped bringing my playmates around because Ma would always go into wedding planner mode.

"What do you mean, Pop?" I asked, trying to deflect the question.

"What I mean is, who had your attention today other than thus, saith the Lord?"

"Ah, Pop, it's not even like that. I mean, I was thinking of someone, but you know what I'm saying." I said, hoping he would just let me off the hook, but fat chance.

"Yeah, son, I do know. So who is she?"

I sighed. "Her name is Tamara Reed."

"Her name is pretty. When will you bring her to church and let us meet her?" Ma asked.

"Soon, I promise."

"I don't know about you, Gloria, but I will be glad when he does, cause I get so tired of people dragging their single daughters up to us after church and introducing them as if we don't already know them. Then to top it off, ask us where you and your brother are like we arrange marriages or something."

"I'm sorry, Pop, but you and Ma were blessed to have two handsome, successful sons. Unfortunately, it comes with the territory," I said, popping my collar. "We can't help it if the ladies love us," I laughed.

"Y'all can't help it, all right. I'll tell you what, if you don't bring this new girl to church soon, I will raffle off your cell phone number for the youth's scholarship fund. I know that will bring in a hefty dollar," he laughed. "Yeah, buddy. We would make fundraising history with that one. Yes Suh, over a million dollars made within the hour. Some folks would take out payday loans and second mortgages just to get those seven digits. We'd probably have enough money to send these kids to college twice. Watch and see."

"No need, Pop, she'll be there. I have finally found the one. Don't be shocked by the admission, but it's true." I told them, laughing at the shock on both of their faces.

"Really, Benji," Ma asked, smiling. I can see the wheels in her pretty head turning. I bet she had a catering company on speed dial.

"Yes, ma'am. She's very special, and I can't wait for both of you to meet her. I know I have a good thing, and I plan to do all I can to make Tamara happy." I told my parents all about her and promised to bring Tamara to church next Sunday.

After sharing a meal with my parents, I returned home and thought about my situation. The task before me wasn't hard, but the outcome could be dramatic. I knew Stacey could be a drama queen, but she was my past. Tamara was my future. She possessed everything I ever wanted and needed.

At first, when I met Tamara, I wanted to take things really slow. "Take your time. No need to rush," is what I kept trying to tell myself, but once I fell in love with her, it was a done deal. I didn't need or want anyone else. She's smart and beautiful. I fell in love with her sexy almond-shaped eyes first and then her devilish dimples second. There were no words I could possibly form to express how I felt when I first met her. Tamara's skin tone reminded me of honey, the sweetest shade of brown with golden undertones, and whether she knew it or not, her lips begged me to kiss them. She had a body so bangin, that she'd make an hourglass jealous-a perfect ten with curves galore and legs that went on for days. I knew I would make her mine forever once I got a chance to be with her. She was the only woman for me, but before I could be hers exclusively, I had to end things with Stacey.

It's not going to be easy. I tried to call it off with her once before. That didn't last too long because she knew what I liked. Stacey had developed feelings for me. Even though we agreed on the type of relationship we would have, she had a change of plans. Just the thought of going through this again with her was causing me to have a headache, but I love Tamara too much not to. I would do whatever it took to secure our future. I picked up the phone and dialed Stacey's number. When she answered, I took a deep breath and then spoke.

"Stacey, it's me. I need to see you. It's important. Can I come by?"

"You know my door is always open to you. Just come on over. Besides, I was just thinking about you. It's such a pretty day. I thought you might want to do something outdoors like a picnic, or maybe we can keep it indoors. I'll let you decide when you get here," She said.

"I won't be there long. I'll see you in twenty minutes. Bye," I said before hanging up.

A part of me wishes I didn't have to do this face-to-face. Stacey didn't have the slightest idea of what was about to happen. I didn't make it a habit to hurt people, but to tell her it was over between us over the phone was not good enough. She had to see that I was serious.

When I arrived, Stacey greeted me at the front door wearing a see-thru teddy. "I decided to keep it inside," she told me, then wrapped her arms around my neck and began to kiss me passionately. I really didn't want to go there with her, this time especially, but seeing her like this just drove me crazy. The physical was never a problem. On the contrary, it was the basis of our so-called "special friendship." And with us, one thing always led to another.

Just dumb . . . I thought of myself as I lay there with my hands covering my face, asking myself why. I felt so guilty for what I had just allowed to happen that I sat up to look around the floor for my clothes. I had to finish what I originally came there for, no matter how uncomfortable it was going to be. I allowed myself to become sidetracked once, but never again. This had to come to an end. She lifted her head and looked over at me.

"Where are you going," She asked with a look of confusion on her face.

"I'll be right back."

I got out of her bed, grabbed all my belongings, and entered the bathroom. I felt horrible. Talk about dumb decisions. I never intended to sleep with her, but I can't front. Sex with Stacey was amazing. Still, I had to be a man about my business. When I returned, she was sitting on the edge of her bed wearing a short floral chemise robe and a smile. With my head held down, I reentered her bedroom. Under my breath, I apologized. I only took a few steps before Stacey met me midway. I looked into her eyes, held her hands, and I told her as calmly as I could, "I can't see you anymore."

Like a storm of fury, Stacey snapped as she snatched her hands away from me.

"How in the hell you just gon come up in here, make love to me like that, then just tell me that you can't see me anymore?!" She yelled.

"Stacey, I'm sorry. I've been seeing someone else, and I didn't mean for any of this to happen. We just got caught up, and you have to understand. I mean, it's not as if you don't have somebody too. Besides, maybe it's time that you stopped sneaking around on ol' boy?"

"Oh, baby, don't act as if you care now. Especially when you've been sleeping with his fiancée for months."

"**His what?!** Stacey look," I said with irritation. "I'm not going to argue with you. We just need to move on with our lives and let it be at that." I was not about to play this game of going back and forth with her.

"Move on, Benjamin? How am I supposed to do that? He doesn't make me feel the way you do. You know how to touch me, how to hold me, kiss me. I rarely even sleep with him, just because he's not you. So how can you really expect me to move on without you?" She said, full of dramatic movements and gestures and one crocodile tear.

And the Oscar goes to… Now, she's trying to toy with my ego, saying anything for me to buy into her hopes of keeping what we had together. I had to suppress my laughter because she was full of it.

"Then why are you marrying him? That's kind of selfish, don't you think? I mean, you are sleeping with him, wishing it was me, right? Stacey, I'm sorry, but I've got to go."

"Ben, you know you and I are good for each other. So why end this just because you've met someone?"

"You are in a serious relationship with someone else, remember, and besides, I no longer want to be a part of this," I told her, waving my hand back and forth between us.

"I don't want this to be goodbye for us."

"Stacey, I'm sorry, but we can't see each other anymore," I said again.

"Well, I don't want to hear that!" She yelled. "What . . . what if I broke up with him, and just started seeing you? Then could we be together?"

"Stacey, I'm seeing someone, just in case you didn't hear me the first two times."

"I'll give him back his ring and call off the wedding," she said, obviously ignoring me.

"Why would you do that? You obviously loved him enough to accept his proposal."

"Because he's not you!" She shouted.

"Stacey, why are you making this so hard?" I yelled back. I was tired of her yelling at me.

"How hard do you think this is for me? Huh? Don't you get it? I've fallen in love with you!"

"Once again, Stacey. I'm sorry. I hope you'll forgive me one day," I said, turning to leave.

"Wait, before you go, I have one question. Who is she?"

"Excuse me?"

"Who is she? The person that you are leaving me for?!" She shouted.

"Good-bye, Stacey," I said, leaving her bedroom and heading for the front door.

"Fine! Forget you! Get out of my house, and don't you ever say another word to me, as long as you live! I hate you, Benjamin. I hate you!"

I left Stacey screaming at me as I walked out of her life. The first time should have been the last time, but she kept me coming back for more. She knew exactly how to get me off without me saying one word as to how.

We had an understanding from the beginning. We were just good friends with benefits, nothing more nothing less. I didn't get into her personal life, and she didn't get into mine. But when I wanted to see her, I wanted to see her. That's it, no excuses. Stacey played herself. She allowed herself to become caught up. I just sat back and reaped the benefits. Hell, she was the one putting it out there. What was I supposed to say, "No, thank you?"

She was the last dilemma of my past. Now that I have gladly turned over a new leaf, I am no longer looking to divide and conquer new enticing territories. I knew where my heart was, and it was with Tamara, the love of my life.

Chapter 2

STACEY

Someone was banging on my door as if they had lost their ever-loving mind. I was still upset and didn't feel like being bothered.

"Stacey!" Stacey, open this door!"

So, I flung the door wide open and looked at my cousin Jasmine like she was crazy. Not that she cared because she walked right past me.

"What in the hell is going on over here? I could hear cussing and glass breaking next door. You know these walls are paper-thin. What's going on, girl?"

"Ooh! I hate him so much! I hate him."

"Who are you talking about, and what happened?"

"That bastard Benjamin! Ooh, he knew how I felt about him, and he ooh..."

"You need to calm the hell down and tell me what happened?"

"He came by here to tell me he didn't want to see me anymore, but before he told me that crap, he made sure he got his last screw in."

"He did what?!" She shouted. "Girl, if it were me, he wouldn't have made it out the door. Uh-uh, I would probably be in jail right about now. Stop crying, girl. Don't you shed another tear for that son of a nothing. He doesn't deserve them.

"He knew Jasmine . . . I wanted to be with him, and he left me anyway. I hate him." I told her as tears continued to fall down my face.

"Stacey, stop crying. I know you may be hurting, girl, but you are over here crying over someone who wasn't your man to begin with."

"But still, he didn't have to do me like that, Jas.

"That's true, but think of it like this, you had a good time while it lasted. You've traveled and eaten at some of the best places in the country. Now, it's time to cut your losses. If he meant anything to you, and apparently he did, just have a good cry and move on with the rest of your life." She said. "Besides, it's not like you're alone. You got a man and a three-carat diamond ring. Anyway, Ben was something on the side, not the main dish."

"It still hurts, Jas."

"Stacey, you act like he had promised you the world or something. You weren't in a real relationship. Why are you tripping like this?"

"Because I treated him like a king, and he played me!" I yelled. "I did everything he wanted. I took care of him, just as if he was my man. Besides, you can't even fathom how I feel about him."

"Excuse me, Stac, but you said it was nothing to your relationship with him. Now, all of a sudden, he is a dog, and you're heartbroken? I knew you were lying. That's why I called your crazy ass out on it. When you started spending more time with him than Chris, I knew it. Remember when I told your stupid butt to stop acting like his wifey?" She asked in a- I told you so tone.

For this reason, right here is why I didn't want her to know. She could act so high and mighty at times. Standing there with her arms folded giving me an attitude. I am the victim.

"Uh-uh, that's how he was treating me. It was no act. It was giving wifey." I said in my own defense.

"No, you are a little confused, honey. You were playing the role of a wifey. Stacey, did you just hear yourself? The relationship was one of convenience. Clearly, he didn't love you. I need you to stop acting like it was something more than just sex."

Jasmine was getting on my last surviving nerve. I didn't need a lecture. What I needed was for someone to understand where I was coming from. I would kick her rump out of my townhouse if I didn't need her right now.

"He did love me. He loved it when I did all those special things for him, sex included.

"Stacey! I can't believe you would even admit to something like that. Anyway, what I don't understand is why you are acting crazy over someone who you know didn't really love you. Girl, you are my cousin, and I don't want to see you hurt, so please just let this go."

"Tears may be falling now, but this is far from being over. He'll see this again. I will make him regret treating me like some random smash buddy." I said, fighting back my tears with the taste of revenge on my lips.

"Stacey, I don't know what you are about to do, but don't do anything that is going to cause you more pain in the end. Big Mama always said when you dig one ditch, you had better dig two. Just remember that."

Jasmine stayed with me for the rest of the night, helping me clean up all the glass I had broken. After that, we sat around exchanging our worst breakup stories. It helped, but I was still hurting. I'm upset with myself more than anything else 'cause I put myself out there and got used, but I promised to never let anything like this happen to me ever again.

Chapter 3

TAMARA

I was ready for the weekend. I entered the house and

went directly to my bathroom to fill my garden tub up with hot

water and bubble bath. I pinned my hair up, undressed, and

captured a piece of heaven as I soaked. This was the only thing I

knew that could soothe the ills of a long day.

I was feeling so good. The jets massaged my back, and

the fragrance of A Thousand Wishes had me thinking some of

the sweetest thoughts of Ben, especially of how we met. Erica

had introduced us to one another during a New Year's Eve party

at her house. She begged me to come, and I was so glad that she

had. She couldn't wait for us to meet. Erica had been telling me

for a couple of weeks that she wanted me to meet TJ's best

friend, but I wasn't ready to start dating again. I was still trying

to get over my ex Marcus with very little luck. Anyone I had met

at that point would have only been the rebound guy.

Ben's eyes met me first, then his smile, and next his physique. He could have easily been a Calvin Klein model with his body type and chiseled face structure. At first glance, he put me in the mind of Boris Kodjoe, and even though he was casually dressed that night in his crisp white designer button-down shirt, denim jeans, and shoes, it was as if it was tailored made for his body. The boy had me mesmerized. After talking to him, I discovered he was everything that any woman in her right mind could ever ask for in a man. I found him to be very intelligent, ambitious, outgoing, and successful. He had never been married, had no children, and desired to have a family someday … I couldn't believe my luck. We spent the entire evening talking and laughing as if we were two old friends.

We'd counted down the last ten seconds of the New Year together, and I surprisingly welcomed it in with a kiss so passionate that all he had to say was your place or mine. The fireworks may have illuminated the night sky, but it had nothing on the fireworks I felt inside of me.

The next day, I called Erica to share with her what had happened between Ben and me.

"Before I tell you all of my business," I told her. "I have some questions for you, honey. Why didn't you force me to meet Ben sooner?"

"I tried, but you weren't ready to meet anyone just yet. I told you about Ben two weeks after you and Marcus had broken up, remember?"

"Really? You got to give me some credit. That break-up pretty much tore me up. But dang, as fine as that Ben is . . . whew! I could have gotten over Marcus a whole lot sooner, but not really."

Knowing what I know now, a little bit of Ben wouldn't have hurt. I thought to myself.

"Does this mean you are ready to return to the dating scene?"

"I guess so. I mean, it has only been a month and a half since Marcus and I broke up, and it would be good to get some action back into my life because if I had to hear, 'What Do the Lonely Do at Christmas,' one more time, I don't know what I might do."

"Was it that bad?"

"Girl, you don't know the half. Every time I heard that song, I ate something sweet. I'll tell you what the lonely do lady. They gain five pounds, just like I did."

"That wasn't the song's fault. That was your fault. You knew better than to eat all those sweets, and you could have kicked it with me and TJ."

"Un-uh, two is a couple, and three is a crowd, plus seeing the two of you all gitty and stuff would have been too much for me to bear. And anyway, Erica, I couldn't help it. I thought about Marcus every time I heard that damn song."

"Enough about Marcus. Tell me what happened between you and Ben."

I shared with her how we talked a little more and how I thought at first this guy was too good to be true.

"Why is someone as successful and handsome as Ben single?" I asked her.

"Maybe it's because he's very selective in who he dates. You know the gold digger types are out there and on the prowl."

"Well, I ain't saying I'm no gold digger, but I don't mess with no broke, broke. . . you know the rest." I said.

"You are so silly, but I'm being serious, Tam. I mean, he is very successful. Can you imagine how many women are probably throwing themselves at him, left and right, night and day?"

"I see what you are saying, but still."

"Just relax and let nature take its course. Every man is not Marcus, and even he was a nice guy that got caught up."

"Whatever."

"Tamara, that boy tried to send you a Christmas present that you regretfully sent back. You wouldn't talk to him anyway, so..."

"You doggone right! I wouldn't have talked to him because he's a liar and a cheat." I said, interrupting her.

"Tam, you don't know that to be true. First, you refused to listen to him and made it very clear, I might add, that you wanted nothing to do with him. Then you had the nerve to mope around for weeks because he hadn't tried to call you, anyway."

"I can't believe you are sitting on this phone defending Marcus."

"I'm not defending anyone. But don't shut good people out of your life just because you perceive things to be a certain way without understanding the whole situation."

"Fine, can I get back to me and Ben, please? Thank you." I said, rolling my eyes at her even though she couldn't see me.

"Don't get an attitude with me because I'm trying to tell you right."

"Anyway, as I was saying, Ben walked me to my car, and girl, we shared an un-believable kiss."

"Say whaaat, tell me what happened from the beginning because honey, I'm listening."

"As we started walking toward my car, I shivered a little, not knowing it was that noticeable. You know that sexy off-the-shoulder gold sequin sweater I wore was very cute but thin. Even with my wool coat, black leather jeans, and stiletto boots were no match for that frigid air. But girl, I would've dared anybody to tell me I wasn't snatched that night. I was looking and feeling good. Hair down, nails done, yes ma'am," I said.

"Un-huh, yeah, yeah, now get to the good part."

"Anyway, he had wrapped his arms around me and drew me in closer to him, and girl, after one whiff of his cologne, caused me to have more goosebumps than the night's air ever had. He then asked which car was mine. So I pointed it out. He complimented my car taste and said he had looked at an Infiniti Q60 Coupe not long ago. I thanked him and told him it was a gift to myself for all of my hard work. So, as we stood in front of it, he removed his arm from around my shoulders, reached for my hands, and I looked into his eyes. Girl, I could have died at that moment. Because, he said, I really would like to see you again. My schedule isn't as busy because of the holidays, and I was wondering if I could take you to dinner next week if you're free. I told him I would love to. Girl, he could fit me into his schedule anytime. Then he suggested I call him tomorrow and set something up. I agreed, thinking this was the end of our conversation. But then he asked if he could do something he'd wanted to do since the New Year began again."

"Again?"

"Yes, that's what I thought too, but before I could say anything else, he grabbed me around my waist and kissed me. I melted in his arms right then and there. After our kisses intensified and our tongues met, my body responded in ways that it had not in a while. Girrrl, I found myself wrapping my arms around his neck and pulling him closer to me. I knew then I was in trouble."

"See, I tried to get you to meet him sooner, but noo. I bet you'll listen to me the next time. I try to tell you about something good."

"If it's anything as good as him, you won't ever have to tell me twice because I'll already be on it before you can get it out of your mouth good," I told her.

I couldn't wait to see my baby tonight. Erica and I were meeting Ben and TJ at Horizons for dinner and drinks. Horizons was one of the newest clubs here in the heartbeat of the Magic City. Ben, TJ, and two other men were all part owners. I was so excited about tonight because this would be my first time checking it out. I've heard great things about it and couldn't wait to see it for myself. So I got out of the tub and rushed to my closet to pull out something sexy. It was late March, and the night air still held a slight chill in the south.

I will always recall my granny saying to me, "Girl, don't you know cuteness will kill you?" At that time, I was much younger and wanted to be on trend with my outfits. I did, however, learn that cuteness could kill you. Especially if you didn't take better care of yourself by dressing appropriately for the weather, but nevertheless, I had to keep it sexy. I chose to wear my black V-neck bodycon bandage dress that hit my body in all the right places, with my satin black platform peekaboo pumps. I was going to make Ben's heart stop with this one. I decided to wear my shoulder-length hair pulled up in a messy bun. Tonight's make-up consisted of smoky eyelids for dramatics and a nude lip. After double-checking that my hair and make-up were perfect, I put on my knock 'em dead dress and killer heels.

When I heard Erica's car horn, I gave myself one final look in the mirror. Then I grabbed my black knee-length coat just in case I needed it, clutch, keys, and out the door I went.

"Erica, you have perfect timing, girl," I told her as I got into her car.

"Hey, Hun! You are wearing that dress, girl. You better be careful. Once Ben sees you in this, you might get pregnant tonight," she laughed. "Are you ready to get your grown and sexy on?"

"Thank you for talking me into buying it, and to answer your question, Yes, I am. After the day I had, I need to unwind."

"You and I both. I'm so glad it's Friday. I could've kissed the calendar."

"My day wouldn't be so bad if people would carry their own weight for once. I hate it when people leave their work for others to do."

Laughing, Erica said, "I see your favorite person is at it again."

"Girl." I sighed. "Guess how often she has either called off or left early in the last month?"

"How many?"

"She was out for eight days and left early four other times."

"Aren't they watching her?"

"Watching her? Girl, yes, but you can't tell that dummy nothing. I tried to tell her, but she called off again, today. The only reason someone hasn't fired her yet is because of our manager."

"You and your office drama."

"I know. I wouldn't be surprised if they aren't seeing each other. You should just see them flirting. The rumor going around the department is that she has been seen several times coming out of his office adjusting her clothes."

"Isn't he married?"

"Un-huh, with two kids and one on the way, I heard."

"Girl, shut your mouth and keep on talking! You don't work for a bank. You work on a soap opera." Erica said as she parked the car.

"Some people will do anything just to get over, but it won't last too long."

Chapter 4

TAMARA

I was sitting at my desk staring at my blank computer screen, pretending to be busy, but I was really thinking about tomorrow. Last weekend, Erica and I went shopping for Ben's party. She found the cutest dress. I on the other hand had purchased two dresses, but hadn't decided on which one I was going to wear. I had until tonight to decide. I was just glad to have a three-day weekend. I'm off tomorrow, but I might as well not be. I have a hair and nail appointment in the morning. I hope Theresa can get me in and out fast enough to jump in Gwen's chair for a much needed manicure and pedicure.

I was still thinking about what I was going to wear when my phone started ringing. It could only be one person calling me from an internal number, my lazy supervisor. What does she want now, as if I didn't already know?

"Tamara Reed," I said with a little attitude.

"What are you doing?"

I knew it was her. "Sitting here looking busy," I said.

"What's up?"

"Can you please do me a huge favor?"

No! I said to myself. "It all depends," I told her.

"Please, Tamara, I am so sick."

Yeah, right, I thought. "Don't tell me you got that flu bug, too?" I asked sarcastically.

"I don't know if it's that or something I ate, but can you cover for me?"

No, is what I wanted to say. "Sure, just stay out of my office. I don't want to be sick. I have big plans tomorrow night."

"If anyone calls or comes by after I leave, tell them I went home ill." She said pitifully.

"Hope you feel better," I said in a dry tone.

"Thanks, Tamara, bye."

I hung up the phone, shaking my head. I knew Terrance didn't know she was leaving. I could tell. Normally, she would say he knows she's leaving, but not this time. I wished I had her job, but what am I talking about? I do have it. She has the title and money, and I have the duties. But stupid me was always picking up the slack, not wanting us to get behind. She can get on my nerves sometimes, thinking she's so slick. I know what she's trying to do, too. She's waiting for him to go to lunch first, but Terrance doesn't go to lunch for another hour or so.

We had three people out sick with the flu, and she is leaving. If she doesn't get into trouble for this, I know something. A remainder email was just sent out to us asking everyone to refrain from reporting off if it had not been pre-scheduled or an emergency. Disciplinary action will follow as a direct result of taking unscheduled time off. I was reading the email the entire time that we were on the phone. It's too bad I won't be here tomorrow because Terrance will be doing the time sheets. I would love to be here when he sees she's left early again.

I will have to call Lisa and have her be on the lookout. I don't want to miss a single thing. My office was right across from my supervisor's, and Lisa's was right across from Terrance's, our department manager. So, whatever I couldn't see, I knew she could, and vice versa. I was just about to call Lisa when my cell phone started vibrating. I looked at the caller ID, and a big smile came across my face. I answered the phone in my most seductive voice.

"Tamara Reed."

"Ooh, may I speak to the sexiest woman alive?"

"Speaking." I giggled.

"Are you busy?"

"I'm never too busy for the sexiest man alive."

"Could a tall, caramel, and handsome brother take you out for lunch today?"

"Mmm, that does sound good. Do you know where my office is?"

"Not really. I know you work for a bank, but the name of it escapes me."

"I work at Yeldon Bank and Trust, the corporate office, and it's located on 1st Avenue North."

"That sounds vaguely familiar, but let me catch this call, and I'll see you around twelve."

"I can hardly wait."

"Try not to work too hard."

"Trust me. I won't." We both laughed."

"See you later, sweetheart."

I loved spending time with Ben. He had been so patient with me. Despite how wonderful our first few dates were, I was still very guarded. Especially since I knew I liked him so much, so fast. I knew I was giving him a hard time, but that was short-lived. Once I let down my guard and opened my heart, his nurturing spirit was all I needed to make Marcus a distant memory. Through Ben's actions, he helped me to love again. After all he had done, I couldn't resist falling in love with him.

Even though we have yet to exchange I love you, I knew within my heart that he did.

He had wooed me from day one. Valentine's Day was no exception. He started the day by taking me to breakfast. He told me that this was going to be a day that I would never forget. Then, at every hour, it seemed like a single red stem rose was sent to me with a note. Each note told of his feelings for me. By that afternoon, I had four single deliveries by the same florist.

"Someone sure loves you," the delivery guy said. All I could do was laugh.

"Nah, I just think he likes me a little bit," I responded.

The last note delivered told me to be ready to leave work at three. Little did I know he would have a limo waiting to pick me up. In the back of the limo, I discovered another rose and a note. The note read.

Today is your day to

be pampered, dazzled,

and romanced.

Love,

Ben

The driver took me to Ross Bridge Resort and Spa. I received the works from head to toe. After my massage, I was told that it was time to check into my room. By now, I was totally swept off my feet. I opened the door to find another single rose lying on my pillow. There was an overnight bag sitting on the bed, along with two wrapped gift boxes. I opened the overnight bag first and found my personal things from home. I wondered how he got into my house, but then I realized how, Erica. She helped him to plan this entire thing. I was going to give her an ear full because she could have told me what he was planning to do. How was she going to keep secrets from her bestie? I thought while smiling from ear to ear. I opened the first box to discover a beautiful evening gown, and in the second box were shoes and a handbag to match.

This man had pulled out all of the stops. When I took the dress out of the box, another note was lying on the bottom of it.

It gave me instructions on when to be ready, but no other information. I had to meet him at eight o'clock, but where? It was now a quarter to seven. I didn't want to rush to get dressed, but I wanted to be picture-perfect for him. A single knock was at my door, and another note was slid under it. It was now ten minutes until eight. I read the message that said to meet him in the Tower Suites. By this time, I was both excited and nervous, and I couldn't wait until I saw him.

When I reached the floor, I was surprised to be greeted by a bellman. He told me to follow the trail of rose petals until I reached my destination. The suite took my breath away. The room was dimly lit with illuminating candles. In the background played the softest music, and a full panoramic view of the night's sky full of stars to add to the ambiance. I continued to follow the trail of roses until I reached Ben. He wore a black tux, and was holding the last single rose to complete my dozen. I jumped into his arms and kissed him passionately, I almost forgot that we weren't alone.

After dinner was served, the waiter left us alone for our evening. Again, he told me I was everything he had ever wanted in a woman. By this time, I was so overwhelmed. I had tears running down my face. "No one has ever made me feel so special," I told him. He wiped away my tears, kissed me on the cheek, and asked me to dance with him. We danced to the most sensual jazz that I'd ever heard. That night, I was ready, willing, and able to give him every piece of me. I wanted to show him my gratitude for everything he had done. Our kisses went from sweet pecks to uncontrollable passion within seconds.

I removed Ben's tux jacket, loosened up his tie, and was working on unbuttoning his shirt when he stopped me by grabbing my hands and kissing them slowly. He looked into my eyes and said, "There is nothing in this world I would rather do right now than make love to you. Woman, I want you so bad that it hurts, but I would rather wait until we have known each other for a while. I don't ever want you to think that giving yourself to me is a requirement just because I've done something special for you. You mean too much to me for that. I'm not in a hurry. When it's our time, it will be our time. If it's okay with you, I'd like to take our relationship to the next level."

Confusion must have crossed my face because making love was my next step. But he continued, "I am talking about getting to know each other mentally, emotionally, spiritually, and then physically." I was in awe of him. I fell deeply in love with him right then and there.

I had to stop thinking about Ben before strongly suggested that we skip lunch and head straight for dessert because I didn't know how long I could hold out. "Now, what was I about to do?" I said out loud as I began to fan myself. "Oh yeah! Call Lisa." My supervisor jogged my memory when I saw her tipping out of her office.

Chapter 5

BENJAMIN

Yeldon Bank and Trust sounded so familiar, but why? I guess it will come to me sooner or later. All I could think about was seeing Tamara. I didn't think I could control myself when I saw her in that black dress she had worn last weekend. I asked her what she was trying to do to me, give me a heart attack, or make me pluck out every guy's eyes I saw drinking up her figure. She looked so sexy, but to me, she always is, even when she's not trying to be. She is the prettiest woman I've ever seen, and I'm so glad that she's mine.

Walking into the lobby, I received the shock of my life. What in the hell is she doing here? I started to turn around and walk back out, but it was too late. She had seen me. So many questions ran through my mind at once. Ah, man, how could I have forgotten that Stacey worked for this bank, too? What if she knew Tamara? Because the last thing I wanted was for Stacey to run to Tamara and tell her about our past. My heart felt like it was about to leap out of my chest. I needed to calm down. The look on Stacey's face was that of hatred, and now she was headed in my direction. I didn't want to cause a scene. Especially since Tamara worked here too, so I was going to speak first, but she beat me to it.

"Long time no see." She said with a smirk on her face.

"Hi Stacey, how have you been?" I asked as if I really cared.

"Fine, Ben. How about you?"

"I'm good-thanks for asking," I said, looking around nervously.

"So, I hear that your company is having its annual party tomorrow night?"

"Yeah, it is our way of saying thank you to all of our employees and investors."

"Is it for employees and investors only, or can anyone attend?"

"I'm sorry, it's by special invite only." I lied. Why was she interested, anyway?

"Really?" She said, sucking her teeth. "My invitation must have gotten lost in the mail." She said sarcastically. "Well, I hate to hit and run. Oops, I meant chat, but I'm sure you know how that is. Maybe I'll see you around?"

"I doubt it," I said under my breath as she pushed past me and out the glass doors.

What a difference a few months makes. We had gone from pleasantry to hate within seconds. I had to get my mind right. I was about to meet Tamara, and I didn't want her to see me frustrated, I thought to myself as I sat in one of these wingback chairs in the lobby. The gold elevator doors opened and out walked Tamara. She was looking sexy as usual, but she somehow keeps it classy and sophisticated. And today was no different. I love that she was wearing a fitted skirt, blouse, and stiletto heels, showing off all the wonderful curves I love. I greeted her with the hugest hug and kiss imaginable. Before whisking her off to lunch, I looked around to ensure Stacey wasn't out somewhere lurking. That was the last thing I needed. Tamara must have sensed my frustration. I was horrible at trying to conceal my feelings.

"Is everything okay? You are kind of quiet. What's wrong?" She asked as we were being seated at our table.

"Nothing, sweetheart. I'm just happy to be here with you."

"You are so sweet."

"So what will you wear for me tomorrow night, beautiful?" I said, needing to change the subject.

"Not sure yet. It's up in the air." She said, laughing.

"Huh? What does that mean?"

"Well, yes, I know what I'm wearing, but I'm not exactly sure which dress I want to wear yet."

"Whatever you decide to wear, I know you will be beautiful because you are already sexy."

"Do you really think I'm sexy?" She looked at me with a devilish grin.

"I don't just think it," I said, leaning forward and putting my elbows on the table. "I know it," I said, winking at her while biting my bottom lip. I was trying hard not to stare at her body. We had been flirting and teasing each other quite a bit, and since we hadn't been intimate yet, I wanted to show her physically what she meant to me in the worst way. But, oooh, she just don't know. I was one question away from asking her to call off for the rest of the day. The bulge in my pants reminded me that it had been way too long since it had some action, and if I didn't see any soon, my jewels would turn blue.

Tamara pulled me out of my thoughts when she asked why I hadn't eaten much. I had taken Tamara to one of her favorite restaurants, Anthony's. It was an Italian bistro not too far from where she worked. They made the absolute best lasagna, but I wasn't hungry. My plate was full. Not so much by food as it was the idea of Tamara possibly knowing Stacey. I had to find a way to ensure Tamara didn't find out about what happened between Stacey and me. I didn't want her to think that I had cheated on her, but made a horrible mistake. I had my future to protect.

Chapter 6

STACEY

"Umph, I see life for some still goes on," I said aloud as I sat at my desk reading a post from H&G Investment's social media about their party tonight at Horizons, which, by the way, was open to the public. I drove home like a bat out of hell yesterday with several questions going through my mind after seeing Ben. As long as I've known him, that bastard has never come to my place of employment. Hell, I doubted if he even knew where it even was. Besides, it's not as if Yeldon Bank is a large corporation. It is actually one of the smallest. So what business would he have here? It had been months since I'd last seen him. Yet, I still couldn't believe how he played me. He had me messed up if he thought I would forgive that cold-hearted mess, but it's okay. I understand how the game goes now. All he wanted to do was get his rocks off and go. That's fine. His day is coming, and it's coming soon. I will hit him where I know it will hurt the most. Our last meeting may have been for his pleasure, but the next meeting will be for his pain.

It wouldn't have been so bad for me had we not slept together. Sure, I knew I couldn't have him forever, but to sleep with someone and then say, by the way, we can't see each other anymore, really? He didn't have to do me like that. The last time Ben and I were together before all of this ever happened, he had really put it down. I mean, I knew it was selfish of me to have a relationship with two different men, but it was for two different reasons. I loved Chris wholeheartedly, but he wasn't Ben in bed. Not to take anything away from Chris because he made up what he lacked in one area with his lips and tongue in others.

I was going to enjoy seeing Ben suffer the same type of heartbreaking pain he had caused me. I wanted to look my very best when Ben got his because whether his lying ass knew it or not, I was coming to that party invited by him or not. It was going to be on and popping as soon as I got there. I thought about leaving work early today, but somebody might say something if I left. My staff was down by two people. It's not my fault that they're out with the flu. There's nothing going on here anyway, and I needed to get going. But just in case, let me see if I can get Tamara to look after things while I'm gone. Shoot, I just remembered she wasn't here today either. Now, what am I going to do?

I'm surprised little Miss Sunshine took a day off. She's always here. I guess I will have to deal with Terrance's BS today. With him, it would be easy. I always used what I had to get the things I wanted. I didn't feel like answering all his questions. We may have been seeing each other or whatever, but he wasn't my man like that. I didn't owe him any explanations. At one time, I had three types of men in my life. Ben was for pleasure, Terrance for business, and Chris for love. That was until I got a little too caught up in my pleasure, and mistook Ben's attention for being more than what it was. Instead of us being lovers and friends, we're now strangers and enemies.

I took a deep breath before knocking on Terrance's office door.

"Come in."

Alright, girls, perk up. I said while unbuttoning two buttons and arching my back. Here we go.

"Hey there. What are you doing?" I said sweetly. Candy had nothing on me.

"Nothing much, just looking over our time sheets. Wassup?"

"I need to leave early today?"

"Again?" He said with a look of disapproval upon his face.

Chapter 7

BENJAMIN

When Phillip and I went into business together, we started our company with two primary principles. Make the best out of what you have and seize the moment. By operating in that manner, we'd become the first major investment firm owned and operated by African Americans under thirty below the Mason-Dixon line. So much had happened for us in such a short period of time. It was almost too hard to believe. I was truly blessed to be able to share my success with family and friends.

I wanted TJ, Erica, and Tamara to know how much I truly appreciated them for being here with me. This was one of the many highs in my life. So, with a lump in my throat, I began to speak.

"I wanted to personally thank each of you for being with me tonight. It is not every day that a man can look out, and see the faces of those who truly love him. Tonight is not only a night of gratitude, but also a celebration. I celebrate my success with all of you. I love you guys." I lifted my glass of champagne to toast them.

"We may not be blood, but we are brothers, and you don't have to thank me. I would have been here, regardless." TJ said, clinking my glass with his.

"Aww, Ben, you are going to make me cry." Erica chimed in.

"I want to thank you, Ben, for allowing me to share this moment with you, and I love you too," Tamara said, kissing me. That was the first time she had ever said those words to me. Hearing her say she loved me made me feel like I was on cloud one hundred ninety-nine.

Tonight was going to be a night to remember for both of us. I can just feel it. We exited the limo and entered Horizons. It was so many people here. I showed my guest to the VIP section, and kissed Tamara before leaving. I went to shake hands and thank people for coming out. I really wished that I didn't have to leave her. All I wanted was to pull my woman on the dance floor and hold her close to me while shutting out the rest of the world. I knew I would get that opportunity later, but it was all about business now.

I saw Phillip standing by, waiting for me to leave. I threw my head up giving him the signal that the plan was now in action. I had Phillip to do me a huge favor. He was making Tamara an offer she couldn't refuse. I had to get her as far away from Stacey as humanly possible. Stacey hadn't done anything, but I couldn't afford to waste any time because of the bad vibes I was getting from her yesterday. All I needed to do was give Phillip a chance to plant the seed.

Phillip and I made great partners. He had a way with people. He could talk a bear into buying a fur coat. I've seen this brother in action, especially with the ladies. He and I have known each other for years. Even though we are great friends now, we weren't always. In college, we were competitors from our academics to our different fraternal organizations all the way down to this one woman that he stole from me, but I'll never admit that openly. He and I became friends when we started working for the same investment firm. At that time, we were only financial advisors. He came to me and said, "You know, with the right financial backing, we could do this ourselves and be our own bosses." I liked the sound of being my own boss. I had only one problem. Where were we going to get the money? Starting our own investment company was hard work. We had to sacrifice and network, and I do mean sacrifice to get here. Every dollar earned went back into the company in the beginning. Now, we were enjoying the fruits of our labor.

As I walked around and greeted our guests, I saw Phillip making his way to the VIP section. I waited until Phillip was talking to Tamara before getting out of her view. I went over to the bar for a shot of Patron. I was praying and trying not to sweat bullets in anticipation of everything working out because my future was at stake. He had to pull this rabbit out of the hat for me.

Chapter 8

TAMARA

I felt like a celebrity, being on the arm of a successful businessman, and now I was in the VIP section popping bottles. I was so glad I chose to wear this dress. It was sexy yet elegant. I knew Ben approved when he couldn't stop looking at me. I wore a sleeveless black knee-length designer dress with a silver beaded mesh overlay. I wore my silver ankle strap stilettos and matching clutch. My makeup was light and fresh. I wore my hair up to give myself a classy look. I looked exactly how I felt, beautiful.

Ben's business partner, Phillip Gray, came over and introduced himself. He talked to TJ and Erica first, and then TJ introduced me to him. Phillip shook my hand, and said he had heard so much about me, and wondered if he could speak to me privately. So, I followed Phillip to an empty table.

"So, I finally get a chance to meet the woman who has stolen my partner's heart." He said, smiling and pulling my chair out for me to sit down.

"It is nice to meet you, too," I said, feeling uneasy.

Phillip Gray was very charming and easy on the eyes. His skin was smooth as chocolate. From what I could tell, he appeared to be over six feet tall and athletic. His hair was cut low, followed by his pencil-thin sideburns that connected perfectly to his beard. His demeanor was laid back and easy. I could tell that he liked the finer things in life, and had very little opposition in getting what he so desired. He wore a killer smile, and it didn't help matters. Chocolate is one of my addictions, and I refuse to go to rehab. I tried to keep my body tone professional, regal, and reserved. God help me, was my silent prayer, because this man was a temptation I knew I couldn't handle alone.

"I have a proposition for you." He said in his smooth, baritone voice. It was so seductive.

"Proposition?" I replied nervously. I almost slid out of my chair from the word alone.

"What would it take for you to leave Yeldon Bank and Trust and join our firm? A position has just opened up in our accounting department. We would be honored if you accepted the position of the Financial Reporting Manager." He said, smiling.

Did I hear him correctly? Am I dreaming? I was speechless.

"We would like for you to start as soon as possible. Are you interested?"

After a hard swallow, I said, "I am definitely interested. But I would like to discuss the offer with Ben first."

"Sure, that's understandable." Taking his eyes away from me, he said. "If you would excuse me, I see some prospective investors I would like to speak to before they leave." Standing, he returned his gaze and reached for my hand. "Tamara, I am positive that you would be happy here at H & G. Hopefully, I will hear good news by the night's end. It was very nice meeting you." He said, shaking my hand and then walking away.

He didn't have to ask me twice. I would love to join their company. This position would be an advancement for me, and I would triple my salary. I would've never dreamt of becoming a manager so soon in my career.

Becoming a manager at the age of twenty-seven would be such an accomplishment, but before I agreed to accept this position, I wanted to talk to Ben first. I wanted to know if working together would place a strain on our relationship. It mattered, but at the same time, it didn't. I was going to make the best out of my situation, regardless. This was an opportunity of a lifetime.

I was in awe sitting there thinking about being a member of this firm. There were so many people here. H & G Investments' clientele was very diverse. All races, creeds, and colors filled this room. This was a true reflection of the company's owners.

I saw Ben making his way over to me. He was smiling from ear to ear. He pulled out a chair and sat next to me.

"Are you having fun?" He asked.

"I am having fun. I spoke to Phillip. He told me about the job offer. Why didn't you ask me if I was interested?"

"Well, beautiful, a wise man once said, 'Don't mix business with pleasure.' Besides, I didn't know how you would feel."

"So which one would you rather I be, business or pleasure?"

"I'm not sure. Although I would love to have both relationships with you, it's all about what you want."

"Do you think working so close together may affect us professionally?"

"No, I don't think, I know. Tamara, I'm just sitting next to you, and all I want to do is get you out of that dress."

"If I have my own office and you stay in your office, we won't have any problems."

"That's the problem. I wouldn't want to stay in my office, knowing I could be in yours looking at you every day."

"I hope you know that you can't run a business that way. You know what your problem is, Benjamin Harris? You don't know how to separate business from pleasure. What would you do if we were married and working together?"

"I would be signing papers one minute and getting quickies the next." He said, laughing.

"There is no hope for you. Do you know that?"

"Do you honestly think it could work, Tamara?" He was starting to make me second- guess myself, but more than anything, I knew I could do a great job.

"Yes, but you must keep our work relationship professional."

"Okay then, let's give it a shot. I want you to start first thing Monday morning. Be advised that you will be treated like any other employee. Please use your discretion when it comes to our personal matters. I do not wish to cause any chaos whatsoever. So, will you be okay with the terms and conditions of our working environment?" He asked sternly.

I nodded yes.

He smiled at me. "Tamara, I'm warning you, if we end up in the utility closet and get caught by housekeeping, it's all your fault." He said, laughing.

"You are so silly. I don't know what I am going to do with you."

"I know what you can do with me," he said.

I gave him a funny look.

"What? All I want to do right now is hit the dance floor. I feel like dancing. By the way have I told you, that I loved you, today?"

"No, not to me personally," I told him as he pulled me closer into his arms.

"Well, Tamara Reed, I don't want another second to go by without your knowing that I love you and how happy you have made me, and I plan on making sure you know just how much later on."

"Ooh, I can't wait, and I love you, too." I said, kissing him.

He grabbed my hand and led me to the dance floor. We started dancing to "Between the Sheets" by The Isley Brothers. He held me close, and we were one. I never wanted this moment to ever end. My turn had finally come. Ben promised me that for the rest of the night, it would be me and him, no investors, no employees, no hellos, and no goodbyes. Imagine my disappointment when somebody caused Ben to break his promise. At that point, I gave him his privacy and I left him on the dance floor, talking to whomever it was.

Chapter 9

STACEY

Chris and I had just entered the club. It was packed. I wasn't here to join in the festivities. I had my own show about to take center stage. I scanned the room to see if I could find Ben. He was on the dance floor dancing with some chick. That figured. Poor girl didn't know that when you lay down with a dog, you will soon get up with fleas. Now was the time to drop my bomb. I grabbed Chris by the hand and led him in Ben's direction.

We were finally standing behind Ben. I let go of Chris's hand to stand behind him while he tapped Ben on the shoulder. Whomever he was dancing with had just walked away, mumbling something. I didn't see who she was, but ole girl was better off without him, anyway.

"Yo frat! What's up?" Chris said.

"Oh, my God! Boy, what's up? Why didn't you tell me you were coming down?" They hugged.

"I wanted to surprise my baby brother."

"Ce, you could have told me that you were coming? How long have you been here? Does Ma and Pop know you're here?"

"I got in late last night. I've been so busy getting ready for your big event that I haven't had time to talk to them yet, but I'll get by there before I leave."

"Wait until I tell TJ? He is going to be so surprised to see you?"

"I know. I haven't seen that Joker since Christmas."

"How long are you going to be here?"

"I'm leaving Sunday night but will transfer here in about three weeks. I just hadn't had a chance to talk to you and catch you up on everything. I've been so busy."

"Well, you are here now. Where are you staying? I hope not in a hotel. If so, just be prepared to check out."

"I am staying with my girl. I told you I was getting married, remember?"

"Yeah . . . yeah-but we never did get a chance to talk about her. Hell, I don't even know her name. Is she here with you?" He asked.

Chris told his brother yes and tried to pull me around to Ben, but Ben started talking again before I could move.

"Ce, I want you to meet my girl, too. Y'all follow me so we all can be introduced to each other." Ben said, pulling Chris along.

I grabbed Chris's hand and followed behind them. This was going to be so good. Ben doesn't have the slightest clue. I'm the woman his brother is talking about. We enter the VIP area. I was still standing behind Chris, unable to see anything. All I knew was he had just been introduced to some girl.

"Baby brother, I want you to meet the future, Mrs. Christopher D. Harris." Chris reached behind him, took my hand, and pulled me in front of him. So there I stood, face to face with

Ben. The look on his face was priceless. But, unfortunately, he didn't get a chance to speak because the girl Ben was with called my name. **Wait, Tamara?!**

Chapter 10

BENJAMIN

I had several emotions hit me all at once. I was going to be sick. I am glad Tamara called Stacey's name before I said something. This trick knew the whole damn time that she was sleeping with two brothers. I had to leave. If I didn't, I was going to choke her. I couldn't believe it. She was just standing there smirking as if something was funny. My brother didn't have a clue just how trifflin' she really was. The longer I stood there, the more upset I became. I had to go somewhere to get a drink, quick.

"Hey guys, ah- I'm heading to the bar. Go ahead, help yourselves to some food, and I will be right back."

"Wait. I would like to go with you?" Recognizing the voice, I turned around slowly, ready to spit venom.

"I don't think so," TJ said through his teeth.

"Why not? I need to get better acquainted with my future brother-in-law." She said with an evil grin.

She followed behind me. Instead of going to the bar, I went outside to confront her.

"What kind of jacked-up game are you playing, Stacey?"

"I am not playing any games."

"Why didn't you tell me that you were engaged to my damn brother?!" I said, yelling in her face. At this point, I couldn't help but walk back and forth, afraid that if I stopped walking, I would hit her, and she wasn't worth the jail time or the bad press.

"I didn't get into your personal life, and you didn't get into mine, but when you wanted to see me, you wanted to see me. Those were your rules, not mine, remember?"

"Stacey that is my brother in there. My flesh and blood. Not some random stranger."

"What about you?"

"What about me!?"

"Why didn't you tell me that you were leaving me for little Miss Sunshine, my employee? How am I supposed to work with her, knowing she's where I wanted to be?"

"Don't worry. I fixed that already, besides I didn't know you even knew her."

"It seems we have a problem then, don't we?"

"We don't have a problem," I said through my teeth.

"So, are you saying that you are going to tell them?"

"Tell them what, Stacey? Huh? What we had is o-v-e-r! Just like this stupid conversation. Unlike you, I don't deliberately hurt people!"

"I didn't want to hurt Chris, and I could give two cares about Tamara. But what I can't get over is the way you make it seem like you're the innocent party here."

"Say whatever you want, Stacey. Just go back inside and leave me the hell alone."

"I ain't going nowhere."

"Fine! You will be standing out here talking to yourself because I'm out."

I walked to my limo that was parked out front. Before getting in, I told the driver to go inside and get something to eat. All I wanted to do was be alone with my thoughts and a glass of Hennessy, if not the bottle. I was almost successful with that request until Stacey hopped in and sat across from me.

"You can't avoid me forever, you know." She said. I took a drink and looked at her.

About three months ago, I was knocking her back out. Now, I'm trying my best not to go to jail.

"Ben, I know we can't go back to where we were, but I still miss you." She said as she began to cry. I sat there in silence. "I'm sorry for hurting you, but I wanted to hurt you as badly as you had hurt me." I took another sip and remained silent as she continued, "You can't keep treating me like this. Did I ever mean anything to you?" I poured myself another drink. My Hennessy was kicking in. I had nothing to say to her. She could talk all she wanted. I was finished. "Benjamin, you can't keep doing this to me." She moved forward, kneeling in front of me. She grabbed me around my waist with her head lying against my stomach, crying. I didn't move a muscle, even if I did feel bad for her. "Ben, I did every single thing you asked me, no questions asked. How can you be so coldhearted?" She said, lifting her head and looking at me. I was so buzzed. I didn't care what she was talking about. "I remember when you used to love for me to do this." She unzipped my pants and took me back to a time of pure bliss. I wanted to stop her, but I couldn't. Her lips were speaking my language. My eyes were closed, and I was enjoying every single draw. I sat back, relaxed, and enjoyed myself. In my left hand was my glass of Hen, and my right hand held Stacey's hip to help her balance. I opened my eyes afterward to find her leaving, knowing in my mind that would be the last time I would ever see her again.

Chapter 11

TAMARA

It was Sunday afternoon, and I hadn't heard from Ben since he dropped me off Friday night. My entire Saturday was filled with all types of questions ranging from whether he was upset with me or had I said or done something wrong. It wasn't like him not to check in at least once. The last time I spoke with him was late Friday night. He walked me to my door, kissed me on the cheek, and said he wouldn't be staying and would talk to me later.

I called him on Saturday morning to see if everything was okay because he seemed so withdrawn. I tried to keep from making something out of nothing, but my woman's intuition told me something wasn't right. Talking to Ben would have put my mind at ease, but since he hadn't returned my phone calls, I couldn't help but think the worst.

That was yesterday. I had to remind myself that I was never the type of woman who ran behind any man, and I was not about to start now. Ben had the right to do whatever he wanted. We were not married, but I refused to be in a relationship where I would end up hurt again. I would end it before I would allow that to happen.

Even though Ben had never given me a reason to think he had been unfaithful, I would not go out of my mind worrying about something I had no control over. If he calls, he calls.

Knowing deep down inside my feelings were hurt, I grabbed my purse and keys and left the house. I decided to pay Erica a visit. I knew she would be able to lift my spirit. By the time I reached her place, all I was in the mood for was eating and shopping. Hopefully, she felt the same.

"Well, well, well, look who decided to come visit me today." She said, pretending to be shocked.

"I visit you all the time, hush," I said, laughing at her.

"Not here lately. Since we got us a man, we are a little busy." She said, letting me in. We ended up sitting at her breakfast bar as usual.

"You know it's not like that," I said as I rolled my eyes. "Do you have any Chardonnay?"

"Un-huh, but don't try to change the subject." Handing me a glass of wine, she continued. "Girl, you know we all have been there. We dropped our friends because we got us a new man and fell in love. It's all right, girl. I guess I'll forgive you this time." She said, laughing.

"You know what? You are not funny." I said, trying to fake an attitude.

"Anyway, how about Friday night? Was it on or what?!"

"It was on, but guess what? I got a job offer that night, too."

"A job offer? Tell Ben he doesn't have to pay you for it. You'd gladly give it up for free." She said, laughing.

"Shut up and listen. H & G offered me a position as a Financial Reporting Manager!" I said, screaming.

"Girl, are you serious? Oh my God! My girl is going from Nine West to Louboutin, baby." She said as we high-fived and hugged each other. "Tam, you had better tell me everything, and you bet not skip one single beat."

"You know I was going to tell ya. But, girl, as Ben can say, I was on cloud one hundred ninety-nine." I told her how Phillip approached me with the offer. "I talked to Ben about it, and the rest is history. I start tomorrow morning." I said.

"Tamara, I don't know if I could work around all that fineness. Phillip is so fine. If I wasn't with TJ, gurrl, mmmh. Think I wouldn't, when you know I would. I'd put something on him, baby. But if I keep talking about him, I will have to take a shower and change into a fresh pair of panties. Girl, that man right there can get it."

"I know, right? I thought I was going to have a meltdown myself. He had me saying a small prayer while talking to him, and it's not like my man isn't fine himself, but still. "

"Ben is attractive too, but I don't look at him like that. He's like a brother to me, but that Phillip Gray is of no relation."

"You better watch yourself before TJ hears you," I laughed.

"TJ went to hang with Ben and Ce. He left this morning, girl."

"No wonder Ben hasn't called me. He is with his boys, and there's no telling what they are up to."

"Whenever they get together, we may as well hang it up. I may not see TJ until tomorrow night."

"The three of them really have a good time, huh?"

"Have a good time? Girl, please, when they are together, they have a ball. We are talking about two brothers and a best friend, who are also frat brothers. Girl, it's no telling what they aren't doing, plus Ce is moving here in a couple of weeks. We may never see our men again."

"I don't know. Stacey may not go for any of that."

"I meant to ask you how you knew her. Wait! She gasped. "Hold the hell up." She said, putting her wineglass down. "That's not the same, Stacey? That's your supervisor from the bank, is it!?" She asked, yelling, before covering her mouth in shock.

"The one and only. I was just as shocked as you are right now."

"What a small world. She looked shocked as hell to see you, too. I just thought about something. Isn't she messing around on Ce?"

"Girl, you know I hadn't thought about that until you just mentioned it."

"I don't know what to say behind all of this."

"Well, for Ce's sake, I hope they are just rumors." I said.

"But you said that you've seen her flirting a few times."

"I know, but I can't say anything because I don't have concrete proof. I mean, anybody can flirt . . . right?"

"That's true. Well, I guess you two are going to be relatives."

"How?"

"She is engaged to Ben's brother."

"If anything, she and Ben will be in-laws."

"Girl, please. Ben is ready to give you the security codes for the safe and keys to his house. You will be wearing a five-carat flawless diamond ring, living in his bad three-story brick home in Liberty Park with four bedrooms, three baths, and a three-car garage. Plus popping out two babies and buying one of those fru fru dogs in no time." She said, laughing.

"Erica, clearly, your wine has gone to your head because you don't have a lick of sense."

I could only dream of the day I knew him as my husband and the father of my children. So far, I have known Ben as a gentleman, a friend, and a lover. His intelligence, swagger, charm, and sexiness hooked me from day one. All I knew was that Ben fed into my addiction to sweets, and he was one of my favorite treats. He was that type of caramel that I could sample repeatedly. Ben had it going on from his sun-kissed smooth skin to his hazel-green eyes. But it was his lips that LL Cool J would be jealous of that seduced me. But to taste what I already knew was simply delicious kept me coming back for more.

Erica interrupted my thoughts of Ben by asking if I was ready to go. Erica and I decided to go and do what we did best, shop. Before going home, she and I would hit five stores, eat, and shop at three more. I had to do some damage or anything else I could think of to stop me from showing up at Ben's house wearing a short black trench coat and matching pumps. I didn't want him to know that I was a freak like that, just yet.

Chapter 12

TJ

I should have been listening to Pop preach at the second service since I missed the first one, but instead of doing that, I was at my barbershop on the west side of town, reflecting on the events that took place over the weekend. It amazes me how people can play so many games.

The weekend was a total loss. We planned to kick it all weekend since Ce was in town. Friday night started out with a bang until Stacey came and shocked both Ben and I. Then, Saturday morning we all hooked up at Ben's house. I thought we were about to get it up when Ce told us Stacey had confessed to being unfaithful and gave him back his ring. I, for one, was happy, but Ben was upset because he knew he was the cause of his brother's pain. They are close, but not that freakin' close to be sharing the same woman. It went downhill from there. We didn't go out as planned, so Phillip and I went to the liquor store, racked up, and grabbed some grub. We basically drank our Saturday away. My boys were hurting due to the same woman for different reasons, and I didn't like that. This should have been our weekend to remember, not to forget.

Ben and I had been best friends since our freshmen year in high school. Ce was two years older than we were, but that didn't stop him from taking us under his wing. After graduating high school, Ben convinced me to go to college. I had planned to cut hair and work in my family's barbershop, but Ben told me that college would change my life, and it had. Ce had pledged the oldest Black Greek-lettered fraternity, and we went wherever they went. I remember wanting to be a part of their fraternity. All I saw at first was the attention they received from the ladies, partying, and stepping. I thought it was living the life, but when we started attending some of Ce's organization functions, I learned that this fraternity was much more than I could have imagined. It was a true brotherhood. So when the opportunity came, Ben and I pledged together without a doubt in our minds, and we have been actively supporting our fraternity ever since.

We had a lot of good times. Phillip and I were cool with each other even before he and Ben. Phillip was an arrogant, pretty boy who had pledged a different fraternity than our own, but I didn't hold that against him. He was cool and laid back, but I was ice cold. I had to give the boy his props because he could pull some of the baddest women I'd ever seen. Those were the days. We often laugh about those times as we reminisce on who won the most step shows or who had the baddest chick at the time. Even though Ben would never tell Phillip this, but I knew Phillip had one thing Ben wished he had, Kherington Draker, one of our sorority sisters. Ben would have given one of his lungs to be with that girl, but Phillip beat him to the punch that senior year, and unfortunately, she's still with him to this day. Had Ben been more persistent, he would've had his dream girl. If anyone had asked me, I thought he was crazy for not going for it because she liked Ben as much as Ben liked her, if not more.

Ben is an easygoing person. He is the mellow type to let things roll off his back in order to avoid confrontation. But I am not Ben, and I wanted to know what the hell was going on and why I wasn't told about Stacey's sick love triangle. So I took out my cell and pressed the number sign, then two. Entering someone's name in a cell phone nowadays was a no-no, for obvious reasons.

"Hey, TJ." She said, sounding all innocent.

"Jazzy, why didn't you tell me your cousin was sleeping with both my brothers," I snapped at her.

"What the hell are you talking about?"

"You know! Why didn't your trifflin' ass cousin tell Ben she was engaged to his brother?"

"TJ, I don't know anything about that. Don't call my house with no mess," she said. She was about to make me cuss her out.

"Look, I'm talking about your cousin." I fired back. "She showed up Friday night at my boy's party, on the arm of his brother, of all people, posing as his fiancée. You mean to tell me that you knew nothing about that?" I said in a skeptical tone.

"I don't know anything about that." She said with an attitude.

"Whatever. You would lie for that trifflin trick, anyway. Just tell your cousin to stay the hell away from my people, or else."

"Or else what? Because I don't have to tell my cousin a damn thing. She is a grown-ass woman, who can decide who she chooses to date. If you want her to know something, you tell her."

"It's obvious the broad can't make good decisions because the trick chose to sleep with two brothers. Just nasty and not in a good way either."

"Like I said, she is a . . . grown . . . ass. . .woman, and you betta stop calling my cousin out her name, and I mean that."

"Miss me with that noise you're talking. All I want is for her to leave my boys alone. What she did was messed up. Just because Ben met someone else, she decides to pay him back by using his brother against him. Girl, bye."

"What are you talking about . . . How about your boy running through my cousin, dismissing her like she was some random sneaky link?"

"Well, if Stacey has whore-ish tendencies, what would you expect for him to do?" I meant what I had said. I knew she was lying. She was too heated not to have known what Stacey had done.

"Are you finished?"

"No, I'm not finished," I said, imitating her.

"Well, what is it? Because I don't appreciate you calling my house with this bull."

"Who are you talking to like that?"

"I'm talking to you."

"I will see how much attitude you give me when I get there."

"Okay. If you are coming, come on." She said, giving me a little less attitude because, more than anything, she wanted me there with her.

"Where is my son, anyway?" I asked. I was done talking about that. I knew, she knew something and was just trying to cover for Stacey's trifflin' ass.

"Our son is watching television. Hold on. JJ, Daddy is on the phone. Do you want to talk to Daddy?" I heard her ask in the background. Then, laughing, she says, "TJ, your son does not want to talk to you. Do you want me to get him, anyway?"

"Nah, I'll see both of you later."

He has to be watching cartoons. That's the only thing that could hold his attention like that. He watches cartoons like old ladies watch soap operas.

"Do you have a meeting today?" She asked.

"Yeah, I wanted to talk to my managers about opening up another barbershop."

"Dang, TJ. How many are you trying to have?"

"Enough to stop cutting hair, retire, and for my son to grow up without any worries."

"Heeey, I like the sound of that! And you will be taking care of your baby mama, too? I love it when a good plan comes together."

Now she got jokes. "I'm working on it, but I don't know anything about that baby mama thing."

"Anyway, can you stop and get something for us to eat on your way here?" She asked.

"It all depends," I said seductively.

"Depends on what?" She asked.

Look at her, acting as if she didn't know what I was getting at. So I played right along. "It depends on what you will do for me?"

"Oh yeah... Hmm... Absolutely nothing." She said. "And we would like some KFC, crispy, please and thank you."

"So, I'm supposed to give you my food, but you won't break a brother off a little somethin', somethin'."

"Negro please, times ain't that freakin hard that I gotta get buck naked for some chicken."

I couldn't help but laugh. "Alright, I see. Tell my son I love him and will see y'all soon."

"JJ, your daddy says he loves you. He said that he loves you too, TJ."

"What about you?" I asked her.

"What about me?"

"Don't you love me too?"

"TJ, I love you about as much as you love me." She said with an attitude.

"Okay, I guess I'll see you later then."

"Un-huh, bye."

Jasmine hung up the phone. She might not think so, but I do love her. I love her because she gave me James Tyler Johnson, Jr. She'll always be special to me. We would have been together today if she hadn't accused me of cheating on her with Erica. Erica was a client at the time. We had not developed a relationship or anything. We were just friends. Erica always came into the shop to get her eyebrows arched. Jasmine was seven months pregnant with JJ when she saw Erica and me standing outside talking. She just knew I was cheating, but I wasn't. I got tired of her accusing me all the time. JJ was 16 months old when we decided to break up. It was a mutual agreement. I would take care of my son with whatever he needed and help her, too. That next month, I hooked up with Erica, and it has been that way ever since. I was one man with two families, handlin' my business.

Chapter 13

TAMARA

I was so excited about my new position with the firm that I got up bright and early to listen to one of my favorites while I soaked in the tub. Music speaks to me like no other, and I need it today. Gonna Take a Miracle: The Best of Deniece Williams was my music therapy this morning. Her music speaks to my heart and soul. Niecy knows, is all I can say. When I was going through it, and I didn't think anyone else understood my pain, Niecy did. When I couldn't describe how loving my man felt, Niecy did. When I needed a song of encouragement, Niecy was there. There are very few artists still around today that had that type of effect on people. If I could, I would thank her for knowing. Today was no different. I was embarking on something new and needed my inspiration. I desired to succeed in everything I did, with the understanding of taking one day at a time. The song "Black Butterfly" gave me that extra push I needed to regain my momentum.

I couldn't wait to see Ben this morning. I flew through traffic with ease, still listening to my music. It took me approximately thirty minutes to get to work. I stopped by the receptionist's desk and told her who I was and who I wanted to see. She placed a phone call and told me to have a seat and that someone would be down shortly. Just looking around the lobby, I noticed H & G had really done well. Their entrance was very sophisticated. It put me in the mind of an art gallery. They had marble flooring, high-end leather furniture, and expensive wall decor.

"Good morning, Ms. Reed." He said, walking over to shake my hand. I shook his hand, and noticed that million-dollar smile.

"Good morning, Mr. Gray," I replied.

"If you would follow me, please." We got on the elevator. I looked straight ahead to avoid eye contact and wondered where the hell Ben was. He pushed the button for the eighth floor.

"I know you may have thought that Ben would be the one to meet you this morning, but he won't be in until this afternoon. So I'll be showing you around today. I hope you don't mind," He said, smiling.

"Is everything okay with him?" I said, trying to mask my disappointment.

"Everything is fine."

When the elevator doors opened, I was in awe. My mouth fell open. I thought the lobby was something, but this was just as impressive.

"Do you like what we've done with the place?"

"It is very nice. Who works on this floor?" I asked, looking around.

"We all do. Come let me show you to your office." When Phillip opened that door, I almost fainted.

My office was huge. It was almost too hard to believe.

"I take it that you are satisfied with your office." He said.

I stood there and looked around. It was too much to take in all at once. But, on the other hand, the view of downtown Birmingham was breathtaking.

"Everything is wonderful. I couldn't ask for anything more."

"Never place limitations on yourself." He said, but I couldn't help but to be happy with what I saw. It was more than I could ever ask for.

"We have so much to do today. First, we've got to get you entered in the system, a badge made, and have you meet with your staff. They are on the sixth floor. In your department, you have a second office. It is not as big, and a lot less glamorous than this one. So, are you ready to tackle today's agenda?"

"I am ready to get started, Mr. Gray."

"So that you know, here we are all on first-name basis. We like to make our introduction by calling you by your last name first, and then proceed by calling you by your first. If Ben were here, he would have done the exact same thing. It's kind of our way of inducting you into the H & G family." He smiled.

There goes that smile again. Lord, help me, please.

"Phillip, I am ready to get started. You may lead the way." I said, feeling anxious.

By the time I left H & G, it was a little before twelve. I needed to leave early, anyway. I had to go to the bank, clean my desk out, and turn in my badge and keys. I parked in the visitors' parking lot. When I reached my floor, I took a box from out of the hall storage closet.

My first stop would have been at Lisa's desk, but I had just missed her by a couple of minutes. She had already gone to lunch. I will have to call her later to be filled in on Stacey. I walked past Stacey's office to see if she was in. I wanted to tell her I had resigned, but of course, she wasn't there. Her door was opened, but the lights were off. No one knew I had resigned yet. I called off this morning just in case I didn't leave the firm early enough to come here today. I sat the box on my desk when I noticed the red light flashing on my phone, indicating that a message had been left for me.

"Hello, Tamara, this is Stacey. You may not have gotten a chance to get in, but I wanted to let you know I wasn't coming in today. I left the same message for Terrance. If you don't mind, please look after things in the office for me."

Stacey sounded so bad. I hoped everything was okay with her. But, come to think of it, I didn't see her any more Friday night. We were sitting there, having a good time eating, laughing, and talking. One of the servers came over and handed Ce a note. He read the message and was about to leave until Ben stopped him by asking him where he was going. He told Ben that Stacey was leaving because she wasn't feeling well. Then he said they would hook up later because he needed to go check on her.

I cleared out my desk and boxed up all my items. Then, I knocked on Terrance's door.

"Come in." He said.

"What are you doing here, lady? I thought you called off today?"

"I did. I came in to clear out my desk and turn in my badge and keys."

"Huh, you're what? Why?" He motioned for me to have a seat. I almost laughed out loud. He had the dumbest look on his face. "Did I understand you correctly? You're leaving us. Why?" He said, still looking confused.

"Yeah, I got a job offer that I couldn't refuse."

"Well, I'm happy for you but sad for us. I know you will do well wherever you are." He said, smiling.

"Oh before I forget, I checked my messages, and Stacey said-"

"I already know. She left me the same message." He cut me off before I could finish. The mere mention of her name made him frown.

"Is everything okay with her?" I asked sincerely.

"Who knows? All I know is when she does return, she'll be on probation. And if she is out again, she won't have to worry about coming back."

"That bad, huh?" As if I didn't already know.

"Well, Tamara, this is just between you and me." He said, leaning forward and whispering. "She brought all this stuff on herself. I'm a laid-back cat. You know me. I will work with anybody and try to help you out all I can, but when they start looking at me, I have to start looking at everybody else. She should have been on probation a long time ago. I tried to tell her, and you tried to tell her. How do I know…because she told me you did. So there's no excuse she can use, and I didn't know won't cut it." He said as I listened intently.

It seemed to me that her coochie powers had worn off if he was talking like this.

"Well, that is an unfortunate matter all in itself." I said.

But he wasn't all that innocent. I wanted to ask him so bad if he and Stacey were seeing each other or if he knew she had a fiancé.

"Who are you telling? Just think about this. You ran the office when she was not here, and she was your supervisor. So now I have three people out sick. You just resigned, and now Stacey is hanging out the door by a thread. Please don't forget about me because I may need a job behind all of this."

I tried to withhold my laughter, but I couldn't. Not that his situation was funny, but more so how things have changed for me. "I'm sorry to laugh, but this is so unbelievable. Last week, I was just an assistant supervisor/ Financial Reporting Accountant, and now I am the Financial Reporting Manager," I said, still laughing.

"Tamara, that is amazing. I am so proud of you. I wish you could stay, but I would jump ship too for a better opportunity. When do you start?"

"I started today."

"What! I know you had better not forget about me. I may need to come work for you. What company are you with?"

"Harris and Gray Investment Firm."

"That's a good company. Are they accepting applications because a brother could use an upgrade?"

"Terrance, you are too funny. I am going to miss laughing at you."

"No, you won't. Just call me when you have nothing else better to do."

"I sure will. You can count on it. Well, I am going to leave before you make me cry."

"Ah, girl, give me a hug, and don't forget about the poor and the needy." I hugged him.

"Terrance, the poor and the needy?" I asked, walking out the door.

"Yeah, I'm poor, and they are the needy." He said, pointing at my now ex-coworkers.

I laughed at him until I was out of the building. That was

one for the road. Despite his fooling around with Stacey,

Terrance was a really decent guy. I am going to miss them all,

even Stacey.

***

I wanted to call Erica at work to tell her the latest gossip,

but I left my phone on my desk at H & G. I would lose my head

if it weren't attached. So I made a right turn on Gresham and

headed towards Erica's place of employment. I pulled up in front

of Haden Middle School and parked. I entered the building,

walked into the office, signed the visitor's log, and received my

visitor's badge. The secretary called Erica's classroom for me.

While waiting on Erica, the secretary began to look me up and

down. She was the nosey type, too. She asked me if I was a

parent or if I was from the Board of Education. I replied neither.

The secretary looked to be in her early fifties. She wore no

make-up and had salt and pepper colored hair that was pulled

back in a bun. She wore a floral print dress with a navy blue sweater draped over her shoulders and arms. Her glasses rested on the tip of her nose. Whenever she looked at someone, she would look at them over the rim of her glasses, and to read through her glasses, she tilted her head back. I wondered if she was mean because she sure looked like it. I sat quietly along with a kid who was just sent to the principal's office.

Erica finally brought her butt into the office, and I was so glad to see her that I didn't know what to do. I felt like I was in trouble or something. It was really bad when the student who was in trouble and I wore the same facial expression looking at that lady. I hated leaving the kid behind, but it was either him or me, and I chose myself. So I wished him well and left.

"Hey, girl?" I said as Erica and I hugged.

"How was your big day?" She asked, me smiling.

"It was good. I have so much to tell you, but I left my phone at work. How much time do you have?"

"I have quite a bit. This is my planning period, so we have about forty-five minutes." She said, looking at her watch.

"Good, 'cause telling you everything may take that long."
We walked to Erica's classroom.

She was a seventh-grade Social Studies teacher. Ever since we were kids, she'd always wanted to be a teacher.

"Okay, what happened?" She asked.

"This morning started out with a bang. Guess who I saw, and they showed me around this morning?"

"Ben."

I knew she was going to say that.

"No." I sighed. "Phillip." We were full of giggles now.

"Girl, was he looking sexy?"

"Is that a word you can say on school premises?"

"What word?"

"Sexy."

"Helfa, if you don't answer my question." She laughed.

"Yes, he was. But, Erica, I had to keep my eyes straight ahead. He was in one of those tailored-made Brooks Brothers suits, looking and smelling good."

"Okay, we had better change the subject before I have to go home early."

"Guess whose tail is hanging on by a thread of their Victoria Secrets?"

"Who? No, let me guess, Stacey?"

"Bingo. Terrance told me all about it and said she would be on probation when she returned to work."

"Returned? Are they still on the DL?"

"In so many words, I believe so. He didn't come right out and say, but you know."

"You should know better than anyone. Your office is right across from hers. If you had just come out of your office more often, you might have caught some of that sneaking and creeping going on. Now we have to call Lisa every day."

"I don't know, girl. I'm not that nosey. Besides, I was so busy at times I couldn't catch anything." Then, I noticed her sliding her chair back. "Erica, why are you moving?"

"I'm just trying to clear some space, so when that lightning bolt comes down and strikes you for that lie you just told, it won't hit me."

"Whatever. You are just as nosey as I am," I said, laughing at her.

"What are you guys doing this weekend?"

"Nothing that I know of unless he has a business trip. What do you have planned?"

"I want to cook dinner for us on Saturday."

"What are you trying to cook?" I asked with concern.

"I don't know why you act like that because I can burn in the kitchen," Erica said.

"You can burn alright, everything in sight."

"You would be proud to know that I haven't burned anything in a while. I am planning to make chicken Alfredo with broccoli. It's going to be good, you'll see. I've made it for TJ before, and he liked it." She said with a proud grin on her face.

"Well, since TJ is still in the land of the living, and I didn't have to contact his next of kin, I guess it'll be okay."

"You just make sure you and your man are there Saturday."

Kidding her, I said, "Fine, but I'm bringing the pink stuff just in case."

Laughing, she said, "Whatever, you are trying to front, but you will want seconds, watch."

"Un-huh, you are right and if something happens, I only pray God will give me a second chance to live." Laughing, I continued, "I am going to get out of here. I need to go back to H & G and grab my phone. I will talk to you later."

"Goodbye. Don't let the door hit you where the good Lawd split you."

"Erica, do I detect a little hostility?"

"Nope, not from me. When I fix your plate, I will add something special to your portion."

"I hope it's for the better."

"We'll see?" Erica said, smiling. "Call me later. I would walk you out, but I don't like you that much."

She had walked me halfway up the hall because she had to pick up the little darlings from P.E.

"That's fine. I love you, too. Bye," I told her as I returned to the office to sign out.

Chapter 14

BENJAMIN

I came into work with the worst hangover. I was hoping to catch Tamara, but she had already left. I saw where she had called, but as my great-granddaddy could say, 'I was thrrreeeeww' on Saturday, and Sunday was no better. TJ, Phillip, and I were waiting for Ce to come over so we could discuss our weekend itinerary. I was going to wild out. Finally, I had something to celebrate. Stacey was out, Tamara was in, and all was well until Ce came in looking like someone told him he had less than ten minutes to live. I usually don't drink heavily, but when he said Stacey had been unfaithful, I knew I was the source of his pain. I tried to kill off my guilty conscience with alcohol. I still don't know why I did that to myself. I definitely don't advocate drinking away your problems, hitting women, and something else, but my head hurts too bad to think of the rest. I laid back in my chair and closed my eyes after pulling my shades off with instant regret. The light was not my friend, natural or otherwise. I heard my secretary talking to someone in front of my office door. I wondered who she was talking to so loudly, hoping whoever it was wasn't here to see me . . . too late.

"Benjamin," she said, busting into my office. "I want you to meet our new Financial Reporting Manager, Tamara Reed." I put on my best plastic smile.

"Tamara, this is Benjamin," she said. I stood to shake Tamara's hand.

"Thank you, Ms. Hopkins. I can take it from here. Please have a seat. I was going over some paperwork. I will be right with you." I lied. I was very glad to see her in my heart, but I felt so bad that I wanted to climb under a rock.

"Before I go to lunch, can I get something for you or Tamara?"

"No, thank you." We said in unison while looking at one each other.

"Okay then, Phillip is gone for the day. He had a meeting at Liberty Center. I will return at three." She said.

Ms. Hopkins was such a lovely, respectable older woman. I love that lady. God knows I do, but I wish she'd stop talking to me and leave because I was feeling worse by the minute.

"Thanks, Ms. Hopkins. Have a good lunch." She walked out, closing the door behind her, and as soon as she did, I dropped my head on the desk.

"You look like you're having a great day. What is wrong with you?" Tamara asked, being sarcastic.

"No, baby, I'm not having a great day. My head hurts, and I feel like hell."

"Why does your head hurt so much, as if I didn't already know? Partying like frat boys will cause those problems." She said with a frown on her face and arms folded.

"We weren't partying. Ce told us Stacey called off the engagement. She told him that she couldn't marry him because she had been unfaithful. So we basically helped him cope with his pain."

"So that's why she wasn't at work." I heard her mumble to herself.

"What do you mean she wasn't at work, and how would you know!?" I shouted.

"I had to clean out my desk and turn in my badge and keys. But why are you yelling at me?"

"I'm sorry, sweetheart. My head is killing me, and I'm not thinking right." I was just thankful Stacey wasn't there.

"So, how is he doing?"

"He's the same. He left this morning going home."

"Now I see why you weren't here this morning and didn't call me at all this weekend." She said, frowning, with her arms still folded.

"Baby, I'm so sorry, but I promise I will make it up to you."

"So, how long do you plan on staying here?"

"Until I can get my eyes to accept natural sunlight again."

"Ben, you need to go home."

"I know. I know."

"You need to go home and rest so you can feel better. I don't know what you were thinking. Did you drive yourself to work?"

"No. I had a car to bring me here. Tamara, do you love me? If you do, I need two favors from you. One, stop fussing at me, and two, please take me home."

"Sure. I need to grab my phone first, and I will take you home, but you have not heard the last of this." She said, leaving my office and going into hers.

I closed my eyes again for some much-needed relief.

"Put your shades on so we can go." She said as she returned to my office.

***

The ride home was smooth and peaceful. I let my seat all the way back, closed my eyes, and off to la la land I went. Before I knew it, I was home. My headache was still there, but not as bad.

"Thank you, Tamara, for bringing me home. Aren't you going to stay awhile?" I asked because she had only parked the car and not removed her seatbelt.

"I don't know if I should. You have a hangover. What you need is to lie down."

"No, what I need is a beer," I said, getting out of the car.

"A what? Man, that's what got you into all this trouble, drinking."

"Tamara, don't make me laugh. My head already hurts. You didn't know that drinking a little hair of the dog that bit you would help your hangover go away?" I told her as she exited the car.

"No, but if you're sure about that, go right ahead." She said, following me into the house. I drank my beer to ease my headache. I watched Tamara kick off her shoes. My baby was looking so good in her navy blue suit, and it looked like it was tailor-made to fit her. I hated that I wasn't there to see her this morning. I knew she was upset with me. I could tell by the tension in the air.

"Tamara, I'm going upstairs to lie down."

"Okay, well . . . I'll see you tomorrow, I guess." She reached down to grab her shoes.

"Baby, you don't have to leave. Come up with me and tell me about your day. I want to hear all about it."

Before she could protest, I took her by the hand and led her upstairs to my bedroom. I went into my bathroom, pulled off my clothes, and put on my lounging pants. When I came out, she stood there staring out of the window. I walked up behind her, wrapped my arms around her waist, and held her as tight as I could.

"Are you enjoying the view?" I asked.

"I am. It looks so peaceful. I love nature scenes. I'm glad, for your sake that your view is of the woods. Having floor-to-ceiling windows and no curtains, you would make any peeping Tom happy."

"Don't nobody want to see me in all my splendor but you."

"How do you know? For all I know, there may be some crazy woman camped out just hoping to catch a glimpse of you with nothing on, just as you are now."

"The only woman I want looking at me is you. I have a question for you that is very serious. Are you still upset with me?"

"Very. When you didn't call me this past weekend and then this morning when you weren't there, I was just so disappointed. I didn't know what to think."

"I am so sorry. I promise it won't happen again." I said, kissing the back of her head.

"We never did finish our dance Friday night. Will you dance with me now?" I said, eager to take her mind off of today.

"Dance with you? What about your headache?"

"Gone. Right now, all I want is for you to relax. You need to be freed from your corporate monkey suit. I can give you a T-shirt to wear." She was hesitant. "Come on, work with a brother. Here's the t-shirt, and I will be right back."

I went downstairs to turn on my get-out-of-the-doghouse creation. It will take her from anger to making love in twenty-two minutes and thirty-five seconds flat, guaranteed. When I returned, she was lying across the bed, looking sexy as hell. She was wearing her hair down, my t-shirt, and those heels. Just looking at her made my heart race. Just as it did the first night that I'd laid eyes on her, I asked her for that dance again. I told her to listen closely to every song word for word because I was pouring my heart out through the music. I pulled her close. I purposely played the songs in a specific order, The confession: *Ooo Baby Baby*. The plea: *I Forgot To Be Your Lover*. The declaration: *Adore*. The question: *How Deep Is Your Love?* The persuasion: *Can U Handle It?* The seduction: *Say It.*

While slow dancing to the songs that I knew would set the mood for me. I began to share with Tamara how I wanted to be everything she ever needed and wanted in a man. Then, I led her over to my bed and gently laid her down.

"I fell in love with you from the very first moment our lips touched," I said, lightly stroking her face. She lifted her head to kiss me. I returned to her the same pleasure and intensity given to me. I wanted to share with her all the passion I had bottled up inside. I ran my fingers softly up and down her body. Her sea of moans guided my hands to explore untold treasures, ultimately hitting the jackpot of wetness. I undressed her slowly until every stitch of clothing was replaced by my kisses. I wondered no more if she was as sweet as honey, for I now knew. With every succulent taste, I helped myself. Her body expressed its appreciation, shiver after shiver, moan after moan, and scream after scream.

With my wand, I was her conductor, and her body was my orchestra. We were riding on a crescendo wave of lovemaking, and neither one of us wanted it to end. One quick motion and she was in complete control of me, hardcore rhythmic motions. When Tamara dipped her hips in a swirl-like motion, I almost lost it. I grabbed hold of her hips and held on tight. She was giving me a ride of a lifetime. I regained control and flipped Tamara around to face me. I provided her with everything she was begging me for, all while Maxwell sang, *Whenever, Wherever, Whatever*, how appropriate.

Chapter 15

TAMARA

I was sitting in my office, gazing out my window, thinking about how thankful I was for Ben being in my life. I felt very fortunate because this man could have any woman he wanted, but he chose me. I don't know what I would ever do without him. Not only is our personal relationship going strong, but our professional relationship was going great as well. When I started working with Ben, I thought I would see him at least once daily, but we rarely see each other at work. If we did, it was very brief unless we were having a meeting. I went into Ben's office yesterday to get some afternoon sugar, which is a rarity. Instead of him stopping at sugar, he decided he needed some honey. Ms. Hopkins almost caught us. We had just finished about ten minutes before she came in. It was a good thing that I wore a skirt that day. I like to think that secrecy enhances our relationship. We try to spend at least two to three days out of the week together when he is not traveling. If I wanted, I could travel with him, but I chose to stay here. Besides, I would like him to miss me, just as I miss him now.

Five o'clock was finally upon me, and I was ready to go home. I gathered all my things and headed for the elevator. I looked at Ben's door, wishing he was there. Unfortunately, he left on a business trip yesterday and wouldn't return until Sunday night. I stepped into the elevator and took out my car keys. The elevator stopped on the fourth floor. I stood there waiting for the elevator doors to open when everything I held fell out of my hands. I reached down to pick up my belongings when someone graciously assisted me with my things. Standing, he and I were face to face. "Hello, Tamara," he said. For a moment, I was speechless, but I quickly regained my senses after forcing myself to breathe.

"Hello, Marcus," I said, trying to remember how long it had been since I last saw him.

"It has been a long time, hasn't it?" He asked, as if he read my thoughts, or did my facial expression tell on me.

"Yeah, it certainly has. So what brings you to H & G Investment firm?" I asked, keeping the conversation lite.

"Looking into expanding my portfolio." He said, patting his leather portfolio holder. "However, I am mostly concerned with how you have been."

"I am well, Marcus. I can't complain." The elevator doors chimed to warn of its attempt to close, not realizing that I was still standing in the way, which should have been an indication to run, but no. I moved so the doors could close and placed myself in the farthest corner away from him. "How is it going ... do they still have you working the graveyard shift?" I asked, trying to be cordial.

"I have a better shift, but I am still there in the E.R. Um, Tamara, I know it has been a while, and I was thinking that I would really like to talk to you, maybe over dinner or something?" He said with a look of hope in his eyes.

"I don't think that would be a good idea. We really don't have anything left to talk about,

Marcus," I said, looking down at the floor. He moved closer to me, his hand gently lifted my face, and he kissed me. Instantly, the thoughts of what we once had came back. My body betrayed my better thoughts and began to respond to his advances. He removed his lips from mine and grabbed my hand.

"I know you felt that. You were the woman I fell in love with three years ago, and despite my stupidity, I have never stopped loving you."

I shook my head no and pulled my hand from his. I can't believe he stood there trying to express his love for me. Not now, after it took me so long to get over him. I was not about to backtrack. What I had with Ben was worth more to me than anything else right now.

"I owe you an explanation."

"You don't owe me anything. What's done is done." I said, trying to control my emotions.

"Yes, I do. You didn't give me a chance to explain the last time. Now that you are here, I would like to at least try."

"Believe me. It's not necessary."

"Can I call you tonight, or can you call me? Tamara, you just don't know how many times I wanted to call you, but I knew how badly I hurt you, and I know I was wrong for doing so. I want to make things right between us. Please, call me."

I finally gave in. "Fine, Marcus, but I can't make any promises."

"That's fine. All I want is a chance to talk to you."

The memories of what we had and how he threw it all away stirred in my thoughts. I was reliving all that pain. It was becoming so unbearable. But, Lord, why did this elevator take so long to reach the first floor? I had to get off this elevator before he saw the tears falling that I tried so hard to force back. As the doors finally opened, I moved forward without saying a single word to him. It was all I could do just to hold myself together.

"Tamara, don't forget to call me." He said as I rushed past him.

How could he just show up out of the blue like that, talking about how he still loved me, just when my life was finally back on track? He should have been talking like that months ago. Once I reached my car, I tried to pull myself together and focus on Ben, who was now calling me. I greeted him with a half-hearted hello.

"Hey beautiful, where are you?"

"In the car heading home."

"Is everything okay? You sound kind of upset."

"I'm fine, baby. If I sound down, it's because I miss you so much." I said, clearing my throat and wiping my tears away.

"Aww, aren't you sweet, but you know you can join me anytime."

"Yeah, I know, but I also know that you have work that has to be done, too, so I'll stay here for now."

"Well, if you should change your mind, sweetheart, just let me know."

"I will."

"I'm going to get off the phone now, and I'll call you later. I love you."

"How much?" I asked.

"More than you'll ever know."

"Thank you for loving me so much." Tears of love fell from my eyes.

"What are you thanking me for? You know how I feel about you."

"It just feels good to know that you love me and for showing me how to love again. I love you so much for that."

"Mmm, how 'bout you come see me? I can make it worth your while."

"How so?" I said, playing with him.

"Come to me and see."

"I will not. I know what you want. You just want to get me there and take advantage of me because I'm in love with you. You sure know how to take a beautiful moment and turn it into something dirty."

"Oh really? That's a shame because I was hoping you could take advantage of me?"

"See, uh-un, boy. You ain't ready for this prime time." I said, flirting with him.

"If you are judging me from the last time, I was taking it easy, but if you think you can hang with Superman, then what's up?"

"Not only can I hang with Superman, but I got your kryptonite."

"Drain me, baby, make me weak, please. You're doing all this talking, but are you coming to L.A. or what?"

"Nope," I said, busting his bubble.

"Tamara, why are you playing? Got me all worked up over here for nothing."

"Good for ya. I told you I wasn't coming in the beginning." I said, laughing.

"No problem, because when I get home . . . you will be."

"See, that's why I'm hanging up the phone now. I know you can't get enough of my honey, but you'll have to come see me when you return."

"And I intend to. I'm going to let you go only because I have dinner with some investors in thirty minutes, but I'll call you back later tonight."

"Okay, I love you."

"No, you don't. You just love this big di-"

"Ben! Bye, just bye," I said, hanging up on him. He couldn't say bye for laughing.

As soon as I got home, showered, and relaxed, I planned to call Marcus. I wanted closure for our relationship. It was true that I hadn't allowed him to explain. I figured with closure that I wouldn't feel for him anymore. I wanted to let go of our past and focus on my relationship with Ben. I am very happy, and I wanted more than anything to be free of Marcus. I pulled out my cell and dialed his number.

"Hey Marcus, it's me, Tamara."

"Hey, you." He said with a smile in his voice. "You act as if I wouldn't have known your voice."

"Well, Marcus, it has been a long time." Besides, who knows how many other women he talks to? I thought to myself.

"Yeah, it's been too long. I haven't stopped thinking about you. Tamara, I'm so glad you called. At first, I didn't think that you really would. I noticed how upset you were as you got off the elevator." He said, sounding sincere.

"That's the reason I called. I wanted to hear what you had to say. More than anything, I wanted closure."

"I know. It's something we both need. But, it would be better if we could talk in person."

"You may think so, but I'm seeing someone, and it wouldn't be right to have you over." I told him.

"I understand where you are coming from, but this is something that I must do. I promise not to take too much of your time."

"Fine, Marcus."

"Thank you. I will see you in an hour."

After hanging up with Marcus, I wanted to show him that I still had it going on. He would soon know that his loss was Ben's gain. So I pulled my hair up and sprayed myself with one of my favorite fragrances, *Good Girl Blush*, by Carolina Herrera. I put on a pair of my cut-off distressed jean shorts and a lace tank top and added my Mac's liquid glass lip gloss to finish the touch. Ooh, I couldn't wait until he got here.

Chapter 16

MARCUS

After I rang Tamara's doorbell, it took her a while to answer, but it was worth the wait when she did. She had me at a loss for words. She wore jean shorts that could've doubled for denim panties and a see-thru tank top. When she turned around, I got a full view of something I missed. Her toes were freshly manicured as always, and oh my God, she smelled so good. Not to mention, she was playing slow jams, too. What was she trying to do to me?

"You look good." I told her.

"Thanks, I guess." She said with a sly smile.

"Um, were you going to bed or something?"

"No, you said you were coming by, so I just threw some clothes on."

"Oh . . . do you always dress like this when you have company, or am I someone special?"

"Sorry, but this is how I dress when I relax at home. Is there a problem?" She asked, smirking.

"There's no problem, but being dressed like that, you are about to have one."

"Hmph, I don't think so, but if that's what you think, then oh well."

She knew what she was doing, but I peeped her game when she opened the door. I knew her better than she gave me credit. "If memory serves me correctly, you love Chinese food, and I'm a little hungry. Would you like to order in, or should I take a bite of your apple bottom?"

"I think you better order Chinese food if you're hungry because you'll never get any of this again." She said, crossing her legs.

"Hmm, no problem, Ms. Lady. I'm just trying to see where your mind was."

I thought that was a little humorous since she's the one showing off all the goodies. I don't know why she's trying me.

She should've worn a Mumu dress, pink hair rollers, and a mudpack if she didn't want me to say anything. She knows how I like to get down, but I'll gladly show her if she has forgotten.

"Hey," I said, touching her on the arm, "I will call in the order, and then we can get down to business. I got up and walked into the kitchen as if I still lived there to look for China Garden's phone number, and to my surprise, it was still hanging on the refrigerator in the same place I had left it a few months ago. I placed our orders and walked back into the living room.

"Okay," I said, sitting down. "First, I need you to go and put on something else because I can't honestly sit here and have a heart-to-heart conversation, especially with your being dressed like this. This right here has to go. I know you better than that, and I would very much appreciate it if you could go and ugly up or something."

Laughing, she asked. "Are you serious?"

"Hell yeah, I'm serious. You're talking about you got a man, and when I come over, you're wearing this. Come on, man, give me a break. I'm trying to respect your relationship as hard as it is for me to do. So please uncross those sexy thick legs and change into something else."

"Fine, but when I come back, we are going to have our conversation." She said, getting up to go and change clothes. "I can't believe you can't handle how I'm dressed." She said, intentionally walking slow, swaying her childbearing hips from side to side.

"I can handle it just fine," I said as I stood up and walked up behind her to whisper in her ear. "Our conversation wouldn't have gone in the direction you were hoping for, and as a gentleman, I've already apologized once. I don't intend to apologize again. If you don't change this outfit, we'll be talking about you putting on those do-me pumps and how I plan on getting your legs over my shoulders. Now, what you wanna do? 'Cause baby, I got all night. How about you?" I said, backing up from her. "You betta gon, fair warning," I said lightly, pushing her toward the hallway leading the way to our used-to-be bedroom. "Gon on now, I'm trying to help you out, girl," I said, smacking her on the butt. "That's for teasing me." She turned around and rolled her eyes at me.

When Tamara returned, she wore yoga pants but kept the tank top on. It was still hugging her in all the right places, but hey, it was a compromise. When our food came, we ate, laughed, and talked about our families, friends, and old times. We were really having a good time. I was enjoying every moment I spent with her.

"You know, Tamara, I really do miss this. I've missed you. We haven't laughed and talked like this in like forever."

"Yeah, I know. But unfortunately, Marcus, missing me wouldn't have been a problem had you loved me enough to stay faithful to me." She said, gathering the emptied cartons to take to the kitchen.

"Tamara, that isn't true. I never stopped loving you, and I was always faithful." I yelled to her while she was in the kitchen.

"Well, Marcus, can you explain to me how someone who loves somebody else plans to cheat on them and then lies about it? I was hurt, Marcus. You didn't have the decency to tell me the truth. I at least deserved that. If you wanted to see someone else, you could have just told me." She said, becoming upset.

"And then what, Tamara? Even though that wasn't the case, you would have left me either way, whether I told you the truth or not. I never meant to hurt you, and I admit I made a horrible mistake by lying to you. Please believe me. It wasn't because I didn't love you or that I wanted to cheat because I didn't cheat on you."

"Well, what was it, Marcus . . . huh?"

"Tamara, what happened between us was my fault. I should have told you the truth from the beginning. I was just trying to help somebody out and ended up losing you. But our problems started way before then. I had a lot going on with my internship and working crazy hours. You were also working, and we didn't talk as often as we should have. When we did, it was one argument after another. I believe had I been heard out in the beginning, we wouldn't be in this predicament with both of us hurting." All the resentment she felt for me was staring me in the face.

"So, are you trying to say that your seeking attention elsewhere was my fault?"

"No, Tamara. That's not what I'm saying, and I was not seeking attention, nor did I cheat on you. I'm telling you the truth."

"Marcus, I was lying next to you. **I heard everything!**" She yelled. "How could you do that to me, to us? **All I wanted you to do was tell me the truth, but you looked me in my face and lied, Marcus! I don't think I can ever forgive you for that!**" She said, moving toward the door as to tell me my time was up.

"Tamara, the last thing I wanted to do was to hurt you," I said, standing behind her.

"All I wanted was to tell you the truth, but I knew you wouldn't believe me. Tamara, listen, I never cheated on you. When I gave her my number, I honestly thought it wouldn't be a problem.

It's not what you were thinking." How else could I make her see that I was telling her the truth?

"Marcus, if nothing was going on as you claim, why lie about it?" She asked with her back still turned to me.

"I know. I lied about who she was beca-"

"Because you didn't expect me to find out it was your ex, right?" She said, now facing me.

Looking at the sadness in her eyes made my heart hurt more. I sighed. "Tamara, as sure as I am standing here, I loved you then as I love you now, if not more. I wished none of this had ever happened. After I moved out, I wanted to reach out to you, but I knew you wouldn't talk to me or believe me, and you confirmed that by sending me back your Christmas gift. The package I sent included a gift and a letter trying to explain things the best I could. I decided to let things be when I received my package back unopened. I had given up all hope of ever seeing you again until now."

She could no longer hold back her emotions, and tears began pouring down her face nonstop.

I reached out for her and pulled her into my arms, wanting never to let her go ever again, wanting to kiss her tears away. "Baby, I'm so sorry. . . I'm so, so sorry." I said, holding her. "Please forgive me, please. I should have tried harder for us. Not only did I let you down, but I let us down." I whispered. "All I want is for you to be happy. Even if that means, and it hurts me like hell to say this, but even if it's without me."

Without saying another word, I lifted her chin for a final kiss goodbye. But we ended up having a long, passionate kiss. We didn't stop until I lifted her off her feet to carry her to our old bedroom. I laid her body down so gently. I slowly undressed her as I kissed all the places I missed. Then I removed all my clothing and, before entering her, I asked Tamara if she could forgive me. "Yes," she replied. I entered Tamara's sanctuary, knowing exactly how she loved being made love to. Easy motions with deep plunging forces and tender kisses in between. "Tamara, do you still love me?" I asked as I plunged deeper into her. "Tamara, do you still love me?" I needed to know. She tried to kiss me, but I knew that was a tactic to avoid answering. "Tamara, do you still love me?" I asked as I began to slow up. Making sure she felt every inch of me. "Tell me." "Tell me," I asked as I stroked her deeper.

"Yes. . .ooh yes, Marcus." That's all I wanted to hear. I made sure she was well pleased before I got mine. It took all I had not to release, but I was determined to hear her say she loved me.

As I lay there holding Tamara, I noticed how quiet and distant she seemed to be. I couldn't help but be concerned.

"Tamara, is everything okay?"

"Yes, I'm fine." She said nervously.

I knew she was hiding something from me. "What's on your mind? Why are you so quiet?"

"No reason." She answered slowly.

"I know we didn't plan for this to happen, but I'm glad it did. Now that I know you still do love me, nothing else matters, right?" I waited for reassurance, but none was offered. "So, how long have you and this guy been seeing each other?"

"We've been dating for six months. But how did you know that I was thinking about him?" She asked.

"Don't worry, Tamara, I understand," I told her, but really I didn't. I was more pissed off than anything.

I got up and went into the bathroom. Before turning on the shower, I heard her phone ringing. What is she thinking, I thought as the hot water ran down my skin. She made love to me, told me she loved me, and when it was over, she's thinking about him. This can't be happening. I must make her understand that I love her too much to let her go again. The last time, she didn't give me a chance to explain, but this time I'm not going anywhere. It felt good coming to what I once knew as home. She has kept everything the same way as I remembered it. The only thing missing here was me.

When I got out of the shower, I didn't see Tamara in the bedroom, but I heard her voice. She was in the kitchen talking to my supposed replacement. Unaware of me standing behind her in a towel, I made my presence known. He would also know I was here because Tamara was going to tell him through her moans. I turned Tamara around to face me. I wanted her to see the anger and hurt I felt. Looking her in the eyes, I untied her robe. She tried to close it back and move, but I had her pinned against the counter. I started kissing her on the neck while caressing her body slowly. When I hit her spot, she caved in. Her breathing became heavier as she tried to speak. I knew she was about to explode because of the tension built up in her body. It was just a matter of touch.

"Um . . . um, Ben-" she said, biting her bottom lip. Without another word to him, she hung up the phone, and it fell to the floor.

I dropped my towel and sat her on top of the countertop. It was not about making love. This time, it was all about dominance. No matter who she was with, she'd always be mine. I wanted to beat her insides up so that she would never forget who this belonged to. I had her screaming all kinds of obscenities. She was riding on an orgasm roller coaster. We went from the countertop to the kitchen floor when she was on number three. Her screams made me want to get mine so badly that I couldn't hold it anymore. I released every emotion I felt when I realized she was on the phone with him. I came inside her, hard and strong. Out of breath, we collapsed on the kitchen floor, gasping for much-needed air.

"What was that all about?" She asked.

My facial expression must have told on me. If looks could kill, Tamara would be dead. I wanted to say, "Just having what was rightfully mine." Instead, I kept that little snide

comment to myself. "I wanted you to know that I was serious,

and I don't want to share you with another man. He couldn't

possibly love you as much as I do. You are everything to me,

Tamara, and always will be." I said, pouring out my heart

between huffs and puffs. She reached over and softly rubbed the

side of my face. Our evening ended with us soaking together in a

hot bath with candlelight, and another round of lovemaking. I

held her in my arms until we both fell asleep in our bed, as it

should be.

Chapter 17

TAMARA

I woke up this morning to find Marcus gone. The clock said nine thirty-six. I'm so glad I could work from home if I needed to. I was exhausted. I couldn't drag myself out of bed this morning if I wanted to. I had an unscheduled appointment with Niecy, bath salts, and my garden tub. I soaked and reminisced about how I met Marcus.

Erica had invited me to one of her coworker's birthday parties. When we arrived, I saw this tall, medium-built guy with smooth Hershey skin stepping out of a black Yukon Denali. Marcus was that weak in the knees, fine. The kind of fine that makes you want to high-five his parents because they did that thing right.

People were all over the place laughing, eating, and dancing when we walked in. Erica and I were at the bar when I heard someone say behind us, "Would you like a drink?" I thought whoever it was had been talking to Erica until she said, "Tam, he just asked you what you wanted a drink." So I turned around, and there he stood, Mr. Hershey himself.

"I will have a Cosmo, please," I told the bartender. "Thanks for the drink," I said to him.

"I'm glad you accepted the offer, and you are welcome."

"I don't really think I could deny you anything," I said, trying to get my flirt on.

"Really. Let's start with names first. My name is Marcus. What's yours?"

"Tamara," I said as we shook hands.

"Maybe I'll find out a little later what you can't deny me, but right now, I will settle for a dance after we finish our drinks." He said, smiling.

By the time I could come up with something sassy to say, this chick came over and rudely stood between us. I didn't know what that was about. So, to keep down confusion, I ignored her and said, "I'll see you around." Then, I excused myself and left him with his now obviously pissed-off company.

"Give me a minute, and I'll catch up with you, I promise." He said, looking annoyed.

Nevertheless, Erica and I were having a good time. First, we joined everybody doing the "Wobble," then the DJ played one of my favorite Maze cuts, "Before I Let Go." Before I knew it, I was getting into it when someone grabbed me by the hand and spun me around. I was delighted to see it was Marcus.

"I came to get my dance." He told me.

When we started dancing, I turned back around, and in the famous words of Bey, I let him check up on it, and before long, a slow jam came on. He held me like there was nothing else in this world he'd rather do.

"Tamara, I apologize for the rudeness we experienced earlier."

"That's okay, Marcus. I hope I didn't get you into any trouble."

"No trouble at all. I don't want you to think I am playing games or anything."

"Who was she? I mean, is she your girlfriend or something?"

"No, she is an ex that is on the verge of getting straight cussed out. I am not dating anyone."

"Well, you may want to tell her that because she is standing over there watching us dance," I said, pointing in her direction.

"Good. Let her look. Would you like to give her a show?"

"What do you mean?"

"Follow my lead." I followed his lead and held on tight.

I was a tool in his hands. His hands were all over me. Before I knew it, we were kissing.

"I guess we showed her, huh?" He said as the song went off. Is she still watching?"

"I don't see her anymore."

"Do you mind if I ask you something?" He asked.

"No, go ahead."

"Are you dating anyone?"

"No, I am very single."

"Good. Do you mind if we exchange numbers so that we can get to know each other better?"

I gave him my phone number, and before our breakup, we had been inseparable. The reason I got so upset with Marcus is that his ex-girlfriend tried to come between us from the very beginning. She and Marcus worked at the same hospital. He knew I didn't want him to have anything to do with her. Once I found out she had called that night, I confronted him. He said it was someone else, but I called the number back, and she answered. He was busted. I didn't want to hear anything else he had to say. As far as I was concerned, everything he could have said was a lie.

After forty-five minutes of some much-needed therapy, I went into the kitchen to make breakfast. I found a note on the counter where I had the best sex of my life and read it.

Good morning Sweetheart,

I did not want to wake you. You were sleeping so peacefully. I wanted to let you know that I will be thinking about you, and hopefully, you will do the same about me. I will call you when I get a break. I can't tell you how happy you have made me. I know it will take some time, but I know we will get back what we once had. I love you too much not to try. I will talk to you later.

Love, Marcus

P.S. I took your spare door key to lock the door.

I had placed the note down when someone knocked at my front door.

"Who is it?"

"Burkes Florist, Ma'am. I have a delivery for Tamara Reed."

I opened the door, and to my surprise, someone had sent me a dozen Champagne colored roses. Once I saw them, I knew they had come from Marcus. Before we had broken up, he would always send me my favorite roses. I thanked the delivery man and closed the door. I set the roses down on the sofa table. I opened the card, and its message brought me to tears.

I hope these beautiful roses delight you,

the same as you have delighted me.

I love you.

Love always,

Marcus

My heart crumbled at the thought of telling Marcus that we couldn't be together, but I must.

Chapter 18

BENJAMIN

I stopped by the grocery store to pick up a few things for the weekend when I saw this guy who looked so familiar to me. He looked at me but quickly turned his head. So I went over to speak to him.

"Hey, don't I know you? Your name is Jeremy Billups, right?"

"Yeah, that's right. I didn't think you would remember me."

"Why would you say that, man?" I extended my hand to shake his.

"Most people that are well off have very little to do with people who aren't."

"Nah, man, that's not me. I don't act like that. So how's it going?"

"It's going. I guess. Same ole, same ole."

"I didn't mean to stop you from shopping. I just wanted to say hello. Keep your head up, man, and it was nice seeing you again." I told him, shook his hand again, and finished shopping.

I understood why he felt the way he did, but it still disturbed me. So I paid for my groceries and drove home, still thinking about how success changed some people.

That change was sometimes for the best and other times for the worst. My success was a humbling experience. I was grateful for everything. My parents were middle class, but slipping slowly. It was through their struggle that my eyes were open. As a child, I didn't know how financially bad it had become for them. Both my parents worked every day.

Mom was a teacher, and Pop was a full-time minister. His church wasn't as big as it is now. Not a day went by that we didn't have food on the table to eat or clean clothes on our backs. As I grew older, I understood the art of the domestic survival game. It was a hardship game played in many households. My mother would say, "I will pay the light bill this month and the gas bill next month. That will free up enough money to pay this other utility bill or buy groceries." Playing catch-up was the game's only rule, but it was not enough. A family would lose the game if something got cut off. That meant they would have to scrap up that extra money for another deposit or late fee, plus what was due on the initial bill. Basically, having to come up with extra money they simply did not have.

It was hard then for many families, and I know it is even harder now. When a family has to decide between paying this bill or eating, something is wrong. It is one thing if a person is not doing all they can to help themselves, and another to work hard every day doing everything right and still unable to make ends meet. It is because of this that I support programs to help aid the community. So many people think once they make it out, that's it for them, but that's not true. We should do all we can while we can to help our community. There are people in desperate need and their struggles are real.

***

Arriving home, I pulled my car into the garage. I put up my groceries and took a seat. I traded in my thoughts to unwind and relax a bit. I removed my jacket, loosened my tie, and sat back in my favorite chair to enjoy a glass of Hennessy while listening to some smooth jazz as John Coltrane's sax piped through my speakers. I was in a very sentimental mood. No one knew I was home except one person. When she called me last night, I told her there had been a change in my plans, and I was coming home early. I told her this weekend was going to be about her and me. We wouldn't leave my house for anything, and there weren't going to be any interruptions. As soon as she parks her car in the garage, I will tell her to put her phone on Do Not Disturb. I wanted her full, devoted attention. When she arrives, we will be two people making heaven on earth for an entire weekend. I heard the garage door open. She entered wearing a pearl necklace and a short trench coat with stiletto heels. She changed the music on my audio system, and played

Love Drug by Raheem DeVaughn, as she stripped for me. I had my own private dancer, and I loved every minute of it. She most definitely had me sprung, and I had her open.

Chapter 19

TAMARA

My heart felt for Marcus, it really did, but I can't go back to yesterday. My today offered so much more. All I needed from Marcus, he had already given me. After today, there will be no reason that I should have to talk to or see him ever again. I decided it would be in my best interest to keep my distance. He had been trying to see me for weeks, but I had no intentions of seeing him. Though I had a brief moment when my heart was torn between the two, I knew it was Ben that I needed in my life. My love for Ben outweighed any possibility Marcus and I might have had. I picked up my cell and dialed Marcus's number.

"Hello."

"Hello, Marcus. Were you busy?"

"No, not really. Besides, I'll always make time for you. Even if you don't want it." He said, with a hint of aggravation in his voice.

I cleared my throat. "Marcus, I need to talk to you."

"I'm listening." He snapped back.

"I've been thinking about what happened between us."

"So have I, but you already know how I feel."

"That's what I wanted to discuss. But, Marcus, I'm sorry if I mislead you, but the feelings aren't mutual."

"What are you saying? You said yourself that you loved me."

"Marcus, I loved you, as in use to."

"Tamara, I know you don't feel that way. Can I come by, so we can talk about this face-to-face?"

"No, Marcus."

"Well, how about you come over here?"

"No, Marcus," I said, becoming very frustrated.

"Okay, Tamara. You win. Can we at least meet somewhere? How about the coffee shop?"

After thinking about it, I agreed. "Okay, Marcus. Let's meet at the coffee shop on the Southside, off of twentieth. I will meet you there in twenty minutes. Bye." I hung up before he could say anything else.

The coffee shop was a safe place to meet. I didn't trust myself to be alone with him at my house or his. We pulled up at the same time. Standing outside of our cars, Marcus suggested that we go inside the coffee shop. I declined the offer. All I wanted to do was speak my peace and go. We stood between our cars, facing one another. He stood against his and me against mine.

"Marcus, thank you for meeting me on such short notice."

"It's not a problem, Tamara, but I can't say that I'm happy to be here, not like this, anyway."

"I know, but I had to tell you the truth. I am in love with someone else. Our time has come and gone." I said, looking away from him.

This was harder than I thought it would be. I still loved Marcus very much, and to be honest, I never really stopped, but I knew trusting him again would be too hard to do. So I tried to convince myself that Marcus was now my past and it would be just Ben and me from here on out.

"Tamara, I wished things could've been different, but I understand. I just want you to know that I love you. As I told you before, you will always hold a special place in my heart. I want you to be happy even if it's not with me. I knew when you started to avoid my calls where things were with us. I'll always be there for you if you ever need me." He said, reaching into his pocket. "Here, this belongs to you." He gave me back my spare key. He asked if he could kiss me goodbye. I accepted. He gently kissed my lips while holding me in the warmest embrace. We said our goodbyes. I walked away, got into my car, and drove off before he could see me cry.

I knew I had hurt Marcus. I came here looking for closure, but instead, I ended up with a new dilemma. I kept trying to convince myself on the way here that after seeing him this time it would be all over with, but all I'd done was lie to myself. I am not only still in love with him, but Ben too, and there's nothing I can do about it. If only I hadn't been so stubborn and opened his package, I wouldn't be in this mess now.

Chapter 20

MARCUS

This has to be the worst feeling in the world. I let the best thing in my life walk away not once but twice. I entered the busy coffee shop, found the last table available, and poured myself into a booth. All I wanted was to regain what we once had. Now I'll never get that chance. I hoped whoever she's with makes her extremely happy. I just wished it could've been me to do it.

"Can I take your order, Sir?" The waitress asked, bringing me out of my thoughts.

"Huh-oh, I'm sorry. I will have a mocha latte, light cream, no sugar."

I was so into my own world that I didn't realize that there was a young lady just standing there. She seemed to be looking around for an empty table. "Excuse me, miss, I'm alone, and you can share my table if you want."

"Thank you." She said and smiled at me. "It's pretty crowded in here today."

"Yeah, it normally is." I told her.

She placed her order with the waitress.

"Do you come here often?" I asked, trying to push Tamara out of my mind.

"On occasions. It's only when I want something sinfully delicious. But, then, I have to watch it. This coffee shop gets me into trouble every time. Whoever makes those homemade brownies and those fudge chocolate chip cookies should be arrested for aiding and tempting me into getting fat." We both laughed.

"You look just fine to me," I said as she blushed.

I wasn't trying to be too forward, but the girl had it going on.

"If you don't mind me asking . . . what's your name?"

"My name is Stephanie. What's yours?"

"Marcus."

"It's nice to meet you, Marcus. I was hoping that you would offer me a seat."

"Why is that?" I asked, taking my coffee from our waitress.

"Because I really didn't feel like being alone right now."

"I know the feeling - boyfriend trouble?" I asked.

"Exactly. You?"

"Ex-girlfriend trouble."

"That's a first. Most people I knew that have exes had very little left in common unless there were children or property involved."

"Neither is the case for me. I thought she and I were getting back together, but she chose my replacement."

"Sorry."

"It's okay. As much as I hate losing her, I really do wish her well."

"You are better than me. I wouldn't wish that bastard I'm about to break up with a good day, yet alone a good life." She said, quickly becoming angry.

"Sounds pretty bad."

"It was, but that is about to be behind me. I am starting fresh, and moving on with my life. That's what you should do, too. You know the old saying, 'Out with the old, in with the new." We said in unison, then laughing.

"Stephanie, you have made me laugh and smile. Thank you. I needed that. May I repay you by paying for your coffee today, and maybe coffee in the near future?"

"I would like that, Marcus, but before I do, I have some questions to ask you?"

I wondered what she wanted to know.

"Okay, shoot."

"Do you have a job? Do you have a car? Do you live alone or with your parents or a spouse? Because some of y'all be doing the most these days. Do you have any children? If so, how many? Last question - does mental illness run in your family? These things are all important to know. I don't wish to make the same mistake twice by not asking."

After laughing so hard, I answered all of her questions. She really had brightened my day. I'm not sure where things would go, if anywhere, but she was a welcomed distraction. Stephanie lowered her guard when I told her that I wasn't in the right head or heart space for anything more than friendship. She deserved to be more than just a rebound.

Chapter 21

BENJAMIN

I had just gotten home. It had been a very long day, meetings behind meetings. I didn't get a chance to see my baby at all today. Normally, she would've stuck her head in the door to say hi or something. I planned to call her when I got a chance to unwind. I went into the kitchen to grab a cold one, but my cell rang before I could twist my top off.

What! I know she's tripping. "Hello," I said as dry as I could.

"Hey, how are you doing?" She asked.

"Fine. What's up?" I asked, wanting her to get to the damn point.

"I have something to tell you." She said, sounding serious.

"Something to tell me, like what?" I asked.

She had my full attention.

"Benjamin, I'm pregnant."

It was as if someone had sucked the air out of my lungs.

"You're what!? Wait...what now? When did you find this out, and why are you telling me?" I was in shock and dazed.

"Months ago, and the reason I'm telling you is because it's a very strong possibility that the baby is yours. I didn't tell you at first because I didn't know how to tell you something like this and was afraid of how you might react to the news. I didn't want you to think that I had planned for this to happen." She said, sniffing. "I know you've gone on with your life, and so have I, but this...this is something I couldn't hold anymore. You were bound to find out sooner or later."

"I wouldn't have. It would've been myself if I blamed anyone because I knew better."

Oh my God, what am I going to do now? Tamara is never going to understand this, I thought to myself.

"I just wanted you to know I don't expect anything from you but support for this child." She said.

"I understand, and if the child is mine, there is no question of my taking care of my responsibilities. Where are you now?"

"Home."

"Cool." I hung the phone up.

This pregnancy could ruin my family and break up my relationship if this baby were mine. It would forever tie Stacey and I together. **"Stupid, stupid, stupid!"** I shouted as loud as I could and threw my phone on the sofa. I had to do something fast. I had my future to protect, but first, I needed proof of this so-called pregnancy. So I ran upstairs to change my clothes. I threw on a pair of jeans, a T-shirt, my Timbs, and a fitted cap. I grabbed my helmet, put on my motorcycle jacket and gloves, hopped on my Harley, and sped away.

***

I had to prioritize my life by putting things in their proper place and order. So, I surprised Tamara with a getaway trip to Gatlinburg, Tennessee. This was the first trip we had ever been on together. It was fall, and the air was clean and crisp. The trees had changed to their autumn colors. For miles or as far as the eye could see were shades of reds, golds, and greens. It was so beautiful. Our cabin had all the latest amenities, yet it held onto an old-world charm.

I wanted this evening to be so special for her. I didn't want my baby to lift a single finger. This was her day. I made a fire in the fireplace. I went into the kitchen to look for an ice bucket and two flutes. After finding them, I pulled a bottle of bubbly from the fridge, poured two glasses, and placed the bottle on ice. I reentered the living room with the ice bucket and glasses to find my baby already there getting warm by the fire. She had changed clothes and was wearing one of my T-shirts that left very little to the imagination. Even the glow from the fire told of her silhouette. The only thing left to do was to add the music and ask her to join me on the sofa.

"This is so cozy." She said, sitting snuggled against me. I covered her with a chenille throw.

"I'm just glad we had this opportunity to get away together."

"Thank you for bringing me." She said, smiling.

"Can I share something with you?" I asked.

"Sure." She said, looking at me.

"When we first met, and I know this will sound corny, but hey, it's the truth. I actually thought I had found the greatest thing to ever happen to me and that I really didn't deserve you.

So now here I am with you, and I want you to know that I love you more than life itself." I said and kissed her. I reached into my pocket, got down on one knee, and pulled out the Tiffany Blue box. "Tamara, would you do me the honor of becoming my wife?" I opened the box to reveal a flawless five-carat princess-cut diamond ring in a platinum band setting. She was brought to tears. I waited for my answer.

"Benjamin, I need to tell you something first?" She said, holding her head down. I lifted her chin. "Benjamin, what I have to say is very difficult. Ben, I-"

Before she could say anything else, I kissed her. Tamara pulled away from me.

"Ben, I need to-"

Cutting her off, I spoke, "Tamara, whatever it is that you are about to say, did it take place in the past? And before you answer that, when I say the past, I mean exactly that. I consider anything that took place prior to us entering this cabin, the past. If you can forgive me for my past, then I can forgive you for yours. Can we forgive each other no matter what may have happened?" Tamara shook her head yes. I kissed her and felt relieved.

"Now, can you answer my question? Are you going to take the best thing since sliced bread to be your husband, or what girl?"

"Yes, Benjamin, I will marry you." She said, laughing and crying at the same time. I placed the ring on her finger and kissed her again.

We toasted our engagement and made love to each other as if it were our very first time.

Chapter 22

TAMARA

Ben didn't want a long engagement, so I started planning

for our wedding the next day. I hired a wedding coordinator

because I knew I couldn't afford any mishaps with such short

notice. Our nuptials were going to be held at St. Peter's Baptist

Church, where Ben's father was the pastor. All we needed was a

place for the reception. I hired Anna-Marie McCall of Exquisite

Events, and she was fantastic. Not only did she find the perfect

venue for our reception, but we would also use this place for my

bridal tea. Walking through the two-story manor, I had no idea

this place was as large as it was. The manor had groom and

bridal suites, plus other dressing rooms upstairs. Some rooms

even had private balconies. Downstairs held five huge ballrooms.

The manor was already beautifully decorated. All that was

missing was the bridal party and the guest. Ellington Rose Manor

was perfect. It offered everything from valet parking to

invitations. All I had to do was to select our wedding colors, and they would do the rest. I chose the colors Tiffany blue and pearl, with platinum accents. I was so excited and could not wait to become Mrs. Benjamin D. Harris.

***

Needless to say, I have been very busy. I worked a little later than usual, but I had to tie up all of my loose ends before leaving work today. The wedding rehearsal was in three hours, so I had plenty of time to complete my tasks. Thinking I was all by myself, I cranked up my tunes.

Frankie Beverly, featuring Maze, was belting out a tune about those southern girls. My old school playlist was in full effect. I loved this band. So, instead of sitting down and doing my work like a normal person, I was up dancing. When the song went off, I turned around to return to my desk only to discover Phillip had been standing there watching me the entire time.

"You have some nice moves." He said, smirking.

"I am so embarrassed," I said, wanting to crawl under my desk.

"You have no reason to be. You shouldn't be dancing alone. May I have this moment to dance with the bride-to-be?"

Initially, I was hesitant, but I loved the song and am such a chocolate addict. We started dancing, and I was having a ball.

"Girl, what you know about that Chicago stepping?"

"I know a lot."

"Well, let's see what you can do with this." He said.

I had to admit the boy could move. I was impressed. *While I'm Alone* was now playing.

"You think you are doing something, don't cha?" I asked, teasing him.

"You got that right. I'm a Chicago native born and raised. I know I have the moves, but can you get with it?" He asked.

I took that as a challenge. The song changed. They were now playing *Happy Feelin's*, a slow jam. I thought we would stop dancing, but we didn't, plus I didn't want us to. He drew me in. I wrapped my arms around his neck while he held me around my waist. I hadn't realized how good he smelled until now. He was wearing this cologne called Creed Aventus. I recognized that fragrance from anywhere because Marcus wore it all the time. It smelled so good. I put my head on his shoulder, closed my eyes, and gave him complete control over my body.

When we stopped moving, I opened my eyes and lifted my head, not realizing the song was over. I removed my arms, but he still held me. Now, face to face, without one word, we stared at each other. I thought he was moving in for a kiss, but he paused and excused himself.

Would I have allowed him to if he had? God, I couldn't help it. I felt a strong attraction toward him from the very beginning. Knowing this, I tried to avoid him at all costs. This was not about love but unadulterated raw attraction, and there is a fine line between the two.

My mind instantly became bombarded with all kinds of thoughts. What if he tells Ben, or should I tell Ben, what almost happened? What is going to happen now? I was in a panic. I grabbed all that I could quickly and got the hell out of there. Walking out of my office, I saw Phillip waiting on the elevator. I started to take the stairs, but instead, I stood beside him, looking straight ahead and holding my breath.

"Tamara, I'm sorry for what just happened. It was inappropriate, and please don't worry, it'll never happen again."

"Thanks. You didn't act alone." I said, looking at the floor after we stepped into the elevator. The ride down seemed like an eternity. I was feeling stupid and guilty all at the same time. When the doors opened, I walked out first.

"Well, I guess I will see you at rehearsal tonight." He said. I shook my head yes and walked in the opposite direction.

By this time, I was a ball of nerves. I called Erica and told her what had happened.

"Girl, you did what?"

"I danced with him, and it got a little intense for a moment, and we almost kissed," I said, whispering as if I wasn't in the car alone.

"Two days before your wedding. Are you crazy?" She asked.

"I know. I know. It just sorta happened." I told her nervously.

"How can you sorta almost kiss someone else if that wasn't your intention? I don't get it. But as fine as he is, who could blame you? I know one thing, you better get yourself over here to this church before you don't have a groom to kiss."

"Is everyone there?" I asked, ignoring her last comment.

"Not quite. We're just missing you and sexy chocolate."

"How is Mama acting? Is everything okay with her?"

"Mama Cookie is just fine. She is having a good time, laughing it up with the future in-laws."

"Good, because you know I was worried."

"She's just fine. No one has given her a reason to cut up."

"You know it doesn't take much," I laughed. But it was the truth. "I'm almost there,

Erica. I'll see you in a little bit." I hung up and thought about my mom.

My mother is a sweetheart. She's a loving and caring person who doesn't take anything off of anybody. As a single mother, she raised me to be strong and independent, just as she was. My mother and father divorced when I was five, unfortunately. I was sitting there watching television in the living room when I heard Daddy say, "Cookie, you are a beautiful woman. I love you with all of my heart, but I just can't live with you anymore. You are too controlling.

You have to let a man be a man." He said, pointing his finger at her. "If I continue to let you tell me what to do and how to do it, I might as well wear the dresses, baby, because that's all I would be good for. I ain't no hen-pecked man. I'm a grown man who refuses to be told what to do all the time."

When it came to child support, she said to me, "I am your mother. I don't need a measly hundred dollars a month to raise you. Hell, what is a hundred dollars to a growing child? After a while, you'll need more than that. So here's what I am going to do, little girl. I will take every single sorry dime your father gives you and start a savings account with it. That way, you'll have money saved up for school," and she did just that.

He died seven years later from prostate cancer. When my mother found out, she cried like her whole world had been ripped apart. She loved my daddy dearly, but he just wouldn't allow her to run over him. My mother taught me how to spend money wisely. She worked and saved her way from being a small caterer to running a full-scale catering service and café. She would tell me all the time to never say what you won't do because that's the very thing you'll end up doing.

I learned early on to heed my mother's advice. I remember when I was in elementary school and had a book report to do, but I didn't want to do it because I was watching television. My mother said to me.

"Tammie, turn that television off and go do that book report. Don't make me have to tell you again." She yelled from the kitchen.

"Ahh Ma, do I have to? My favorite TV show is on." I said, whining.

"Do it, whether you want to or not, or I can put something on your butt that'll make you wish you had done it from the very beginning. Now, which one do you want?"

My mother didn't have to lay a hand on me. All she had to do was whoop me with her mouth, and I would straighten up, and still will today.

***

As I pulled up to St. Peter's, I saw Ben standing outside on his phone. He looked upset, so I parked my car quickly to find out what was happening. I prayed that Phillip hadn't told him about our incident.

"Sweetheart, is everything okay?" I said, walking up and kissing him.

"Everything is fine, baby. I was just tying up some loose ends." He said, a little distracted. "Um Tamara . . . never mind, never mind. I won't bother you now."

"It's okay, husband-to-be. Just ask me?" I gave him a peck on the lips.

"Have you seen Phillip today?" My heart started racing.

"Yeah, not too long ago. Why?"

"He has my vows and I need them for rehearsal. I left them at the office, and Phillip went to get them for me."

I saw him alright, I thought.

"Sweetie, why didn't you tell me I could have gotten them for you?"

"Because you're nosey and would've read them. I want you to be surprised." He said, kissing me on the forehead. "Look, here he comes now."

I turned in the direction of Phillip's car.

"I guess we better get inside so we can get started, Mrs. Benjamin D. Harris." He said.

"I love the sound of that."

Once I heard Mrs. Benjamin D. Harris, my nervousness vanished. Nothing else mattered after that.

We all gathered in the church sanctuary for rehearsal.

"Come on, let's get this show on the road before you decide to kis-"

"Erica!" I said, cutting her off.

"What was that she just said?" Ben's mother asked.

"Nothing, Mother Harris," I said, trying to clean up what Erica was about to say. "Erica is just kidding around. Don't pay her any attention." I shot Erica a dirty look that said I was going to get her later. The last thing I want is for Ben's mother to think anything negative about me.

"Okay, everybody, let's take it from the top." Said the wedding coordinator.

After saying my vows to Ben, it made me wish the rehearsal was the real thing. I love him so much, and cannot wait to spend the rest of my life with him. I'm still not sure why we had to rush, but hey, I guess that's what people in love do.

Chapter 23

PHILLIP

I couldn't stop thinking about Tamara. I could still feel the intensity between us. We would make eye contact occasionally and look off. I couldn't believe what almost had happened.

Had I not stopped myself, we probably wouldn't have been here. I knew from meeting Tamara for the very first time that I was attracted to her. But I also knew that she was my partner's girl, which made her off-limits. I could tell that she felt the same for me by how she looked at me. I was disappointed with myself for almost crossing the line. Now working together is going to be extremely difficult.

"So when are you going to make that move and make an honest woman out of Kherington?" Ben asked.

"Oh no, partner, you're the man. Snatching up the very best. What are the rest of us to do?"

"Look and weep. But it's not like you don't have a good woman either now." Ben said, laughing.

"Weep, I shall, but joy will come tomorrow night. Isn't that right, Brother Christopher?" I said, not addressing the second part.

"Yes, yes, all you young men un-huh will find joy, I said joyyyy at Horizons, uh. Tomorrow night, uh. Be reeaaady, uh. I said - be ready with them singles, uh. We gon make a tsunami in the Magic City tomorrow night. Well . . . let the doors of Horizons open, and them girls commence to shaking 'em thangs, unnn-huh." Chris said, imitating their father when he preached. It wasn't enough to imitate their dad. This fool had to add in that shout with the leg out that Deacon Peoples does, which puts you in the mind of Chuck Berry. We laughed so loud and hard that it drew all kinds of attention.

The women looked over at us like we had lost what little minds we had left. They couldn't hear or see what Chris was doing. Probably all they saw were the men standing around in a huddle, laughing. The only man that wasn't over there with us was Pastor Harris, Chris and Ben's father. He was still at the table, eating more peach cobbler.

Like the others, I was standing there laughing and crying all at the same time. Chris hadn't stopped pretending to be preaching yet.

"What are you all over here laughing so hard about?" Tamara asked.

"Nothing, Chris just needs Jesus," I said, wiping my eyes and trying to regain my composure. We went back into the sanctuary for one last rehearsal. We had to stop twice for laughing. Whenever Pastor Harris spoke, somebody would let out a chuckle and cause the rest of us to laugh.

Pastor Harris became very aggravated after a while. "Now look here, fellas, we need to get through the ceremony part. So if you could hold your giggles until afterward, then we'll be able to go home. Gloria, what did they give these boys to drink?" He asked his wife, who had no clue what was going on.

She shrugged her shoulders. "I know we all had tea to drink, but they must've had something stronger. Look at 'em." That made us laugh even harder, and we

would've continued until Ms. Cookie stood up.

"If y'all don't stop all this damn, I mean darn, laughing...Y'all act like, y'all don't know where the hell you are! Act like you got some darn sense, even if you don't! Forgive me, Reverend, go ahead," Ms. Cookie said as she took her seat, mumbling to herself about us having her acting a damn fool up in church.

After that, we straightened up quick, fast, and in a doggone hurry, like we were ten-year old boys again. Ms. Cookie looked and sounded like she didn't play the radio. Like one of those mothers that didn't mind whoopin' some butt. We looked at each other and asked if Ms. Cookie just cussed up in church. I think she forgot where the hell she was, but I wasn't going to say anything about it.

After the rehearsal ended, I noticed Tamara staring at me. I looked back at her. She blushed and turned her head. I smiled, knowing she hadn't forgotten about earlier, either.

Chapter 24

TAMARA

My bridal shower had a cocktail party theme. All the ladies came dressed in their favorite after-five cocktail dresses and heels. I greeted each woman with a gift bag and cocktail. I chose various cocktails and wines to be served throughout the party. The room was decorated with bright, freshly cut flowers that were arranged in different styles for a touch of warmth and comfort. They also used decorative votives and candlesticks to accent the floral centerpieces, including beautiful lace tablecloths and napkins. The food was set up in stations. Each station had something different, from traditional hors d'oeuvres to exotic fruits and charcuterie boards. There was something there for everybody, whether you were dieting or vegan. Every taste bud was met with something delicious and satisfying.

Needless to say, everyone enjoyed themselves, and to make sure my family and friends got home safely, I had a car service to bring me and my guests to Ellington Rose Manor and to carry us home afterward. There were quite a few special presentations given. I acknowledge my wedding party, and to thank them for being there and sharing with me the happiest day of my life, I purchased them all pearl bracelets from Tiffany and Co.

It was nine o'clock that evening when Erica and I came in. Ben was at his bachelor's party, living it up one last time. I could hardly wait to get into the house. I had gifts galore to open, and there was a package sitting on the doorstep addressed to me that came by mail. I set the box down next to the other presents I received. Erica and I changed clothes so that I could start opening gifts. Before I did, Erica wrote down the names of each person who had given me a gift so that I could send them a thank-you card. The first gift I opened was from my Aunt Candi, who had a wedding photo album customized in sterling silver. I opened everything except that box addressed to me. I picked it up and shook it before opening it.

"Who is it from?" Erica asked for the twentieth time.

"I don't know," I said, looking at the label.

"Well, maybe the sender's information is on the inside." I opened the box. Inside the box was a single envelope with writing on it. It said, please read before tomorrow.

"Ben has sent me something," I said to Erica, blushing. I opened the envelope, getting ready to read it. The letter said.

Dear Tamara,

I know this may come to you as a shock.

Benjamin and I have been seeing each other for

months. I am now eight months pregnant. To prove

what I am saying, I enclosed my sonogram

and pictures of him and me when we were in

Las Vegas, Hamptons, New York, and Atlanta.

I'm sorry it had to be done this way. Benjamin has

known for months about my pregnancy but has refused to

tell you.

-Stacey

I looked at the photos and trembled at the sight of them and then cried uncontrollably.

"Tamara, what's wrong?" Erica said, looking confused.

I gave her the letter and pictures.

"Oh, hell no! What tha what. . . he has been sleeping with his brother's fiancée, and now she's pregnant. I am going to get TJ on the phone, and if he knows anything about this, I am dumping his butt tonight!"

"Put down the phone, Erica," I said, trying to wipe my tears.

"What . . . why? Uh-uh, girl. I don't know about you, but I need some answers. We gon get this right here straight tonight, bet on that!" Erica said.

"Let's go to your house. I need to leave. But before I do, I'm going to lay the envelope out so he can see it. There is no way he is going to have a restful night." I gathered my belongings and jumped into Erica's car while trying to fight back my tears.

CHAPTER 25

ERICA

"I'm telling you again, Tam, if TJ knew anything about this, he and I are through." I said as we walked through my front door.

Tamara sat there on the sofa in silence as I fussed and cussed out TJ, who wasn't even there.

"Erica, you cannot blame TJ for any of this. He didn't make Ben stick his thing into anybody."

"You know how close they are. He had to know something. I just know it." I don't put anything past TJ.

"That's not true. I won't let you start something with TJ because of me and Ben," Tamara said sternly.

"Tamara, I just don't believe this." I told her.

"Well, believe it. I should have known something was up. You remember that night at the party when Ben said he was going to the bar, and she wanted to go with him?"

"Yeah, I sure do! I thought that was kind of weird. They were missing for a long time, too. This is some kind of reality show mess." I said, shaking my head.

"Our wedding is tomorrow, and I am here crying because . . . because . . . I can't go through this again. I swear, I can't." She said, crying uncontrollably.

All I could do was comfort her and rub her back.

"Now, I wished you had kissed Phillip. That would have been payback." I said.

"Payback, huh?" She said, sniffling.

"Yeah, because he did it, so why don't you?" I said, releasing her.

She was holding her face in her hands.

"Erica, Ben is not alone in this." She told me.

"I know that trifflin ass Stacey is right there with him."

"No, it's me too. I had been talking about how he cheated on me, but I never thought about me cheating on Ben, too. "

"What are you talking about, too? You cheated on Ben, when and with whom?" I was confused.

"That's because I never told you that I slept with Marcus."

"Marcus, who?" Because I know doggone well, she wasn't talking about her ex. I know not him. Not how hurt she was after they broke up.

"Marcus Tyler." She admitted.

"I know you lying . . . when did you see him?"

"I saw him three months ago. I was leaving work. He said he wanted to talk to me. So I called him up, and he came over. We ate, laughed, and talked."

"Wait a minute. I'm missing something. How did you two end up sleeping together if that's all it was?"

"It was a very emotional meeting. After I finally confronted him, we just let go of everything we had felt, was feeling, and would ever feel. The next thing I knew, we were kissing and ended up in the bedroom - then the kitchen, and back to the bedroom."

"You mean to tell me you saw and slept with Marcus and didn't tell me?" I gasped at the thought of Ben possibly knowing. So I asked, "Wait, do you think Ben somehow found out, and that's why he cheated?"

"I don't think so. Ben couldn't have known. He was on a business trip. I even talked to him while Marcus was there, twice. The point you are missing is that she said she was eight months pregnant. What happened between Marcus and I took place three months ago?"

"This is unfreakinbelievable."

"Who are you telling? Before we got engaged, I tried to tell him about Marcus. He wouldn't let me. Now this!" She said, with tears rolling down her cheeks.

"I'm going into the kitchen to make us some coffee. It is going to be a long night."

Chapter 26

BENJAMIN

I had the ultimate bachelor party. Ce, TJ, Phillip, and the fellows sent me off with a bang. The food was good, the drinks kept coming, and the women were, oh my goodness ... the women were gorgeous, this was Hugh Hefner Playboy's best, gorgeous. I was so worked up that I couldn't wait until our honeymoon. I had to have Tamara tonight in the worst way. I know we agreed that after we announced our engagement, that we would abstain from having sex, but she didn't make it any better by moving in with me three weeks ago. We slept in the same bed together, and I couldn't touch her. I would have gotten lucky after last night's rehearsal dinner, but my dumb butt had to stick to the arrangement. Something had revved up her engine, and she was ready to go right then and there.

That's one of the things I loved about Tamara. She was a freak by nature. It didn't matter to her if we were in a public or private place, a car, or a conference room. She was down for whatever. I hoped she would be home and in the mood when I arrived. TJ was speeding as usual, so I'll definitely be home in no time.

Walking through the front door, I called her name. "Tamara? Baby, are you home?"

Man, no answer. I guess she is still out with her girlfriends. But I see she has been here, though. There were gifts and wrapping paper everywhere. I looked at all the gifts she had received. I saw an envelope that said open this before tomorrow written on it. So, I opened the letter and something fell out. When I saw who the letter was from, I knew exactly what it was about. How evil can one person be? She would stop at nothing to hurt me. I had to remain calm in order to find Tamara. She must know the whole truth. I didn't do anything wrong this time.

Chapter 27

TJ

I had just dropped Ben off at home. We were both headed

home for the same thing, only I would be getting mine, and he

would have to wait until tomorrow night for his. I can't wait to

get home. Who could this be calling me this late at night? My

phone vibrated against my hip. I picked it up to see it was Ben's

face.

"Wassup dawg?" Ben was screaming in my ear.

-

"Man, slow down-what happened?" Wow, Ben was

talking a mile a minute.

-

"Tamara found out about Stacey. How?"

-

"Aww, man! I told you not to mess with that trick. I knew she was trouble when I saw her. Now she's trying to ruin your wedding."

-

"Where's Tamara?"

-

"What do you mean you don't know?"

-

"This is so messed up. You know this is messed up - don't cha? Man, I might be moving in with your ass after tonight because Erica isn't going to believe that I didn't know anything about this man."

-

"Yeah, man - but I'm going to help you! I can't help but too. If they know about you, it's just a matter of time before they find out I knew about it. But that trifflin' Stacey tho-

-

"I'm pulling up in my driveway right now. I think they are both here. Look, man, I'm going ahead and getting off the phone, and when I find something out, I'll call you back.

-

"Naw bruh, don't come over here . . . you might make it worse."

-

"Yeah, yeah. I'll tell her what you said."

-

"Okay-"

-

"Okay-"

-

"Alright, damn!"

-

"Fine."

-

"I know what to say."

"How am I going to fix something if you won't get off my phone so I can go in the house to fix it? Yeah, I will call you back. Bye." I ended the call and threw the phone on the seat. I tried to tell him that the girl was nothing but trouble.

We met up one night with Jasmine and Stacey at Horizons about four years ago on a double date. I had met Jasmine prior. She had come through the shop to get her eyebrows done. Since she didn't have a man, I pursued her. She then introduced us to Stacey. Stacey and Ben started talking to one another, and we all ended up going back to Stacey's house. She and Ben screwed that same night. From that moment, I knew that girl was gon be trouble . . . I knew it. I told him if he wasn't going to mess with her, just let it be that one time and move on. But nooo. He had to stay and linger - now this crazy helfa has sent pictures to the house, causing trouble.

"TJ, who are you out there talking to?" Erica asked.

Not realizing anyone could hear me. I answered, "Nobody, baby. I was talking to myself.

Did y'all have a good time tonight?" I asked, pretending not to know anything as I walked into the house.

"We would have if we hadn't found out that your boy had been cheating?"

"Girl, what are you talking about? What boy?"

"What, boy?" She said, imitating me.

"Yeah, what are you talking about?"

"She's talking about Ben, TJ," Tamara said softly as she entered the living room.

"Ben wouldn't cheat on you, Tamara," I said, looking into her eyes, which reflected hurt and tears. I removed my Yankee-fitted baseball cap, pulled my dreads back, and put them in a ponytail.

I knew this would be one hell of a night right here.

"Oh yeah . . . well then, how is it that your best friend's brother . . . ex- fiancée ended up pregnant, huh? This really is some Maury Povich mess. **She sent pictures TJ. Yo boy is trying to play in my girl's face!"** Erica said, yelling at me and pointing at Tamara.

I ignored Erica as best I could. Then, finally, I said calmly, "Tamara, have you called Ben to see what this is all about?"

"No, I haven't, TJ." She said between sniffles.

"Give him a call. You may be surprised that this is not what you think it is. You may have been all upset for nothing."

"Okay, I'll go upstairs and give him a call now."

It was up to Ben now. Hopefully, she'll hear my boy out.

Now that Tamara has gone upstairs to talk to Ben. I am going to handle Erica's red hot ass. She knows I don't appreciate her clowning me, especially in front of people.

"Erica, what is your problem?"

"You know, doggone well, what my problem is, and don't sit there and act like you are dumb, either?"

"What are you talking about?"

"See what I mean. I know you knew Ben had been seeing Stacey. I can't prove it, but I know you knew!"

"You can't prove anything, but you can accuse me?"

"You doggone, right?"

"But you're wrong about that.

"You two are thick as thieves. I know you knew. I just know it."

"I came home to be with you, and I get railroaded with some craziness. Erica, that's not fair."

"What's not fair is on the eve of Tamara's wedding, she receives a package with a letter and pictures in it from some skank. That's not fair."

Something was telling me this was more about us than it was about Tamara and Ben.

"Erica, what is this really about? It's like you are accusing me of something. But, baby, what is it? Do you think I'm cheating on you?" I asked sincerely.

"I hadn't said that, TJ." She said, looking down, but I knew exactly what she was doing.

"Well, baby, tell me what it is so that I can fix it. I don't want anything to come between us. You know I love you too much for that. Come here. Let me tell you something." I pulled her into my arms. "Listen, there is no one out there that is more important than you. I came home tonight wanting to talk to you about our future."

I knew that was what she has been waiting to hear. We had been together longer than Ben and Tamara, yet they were getting married. She had been snippy with me ever since their engagement had been announced.

"I want to make our relationship permanent. This is not an official proposal. I want to go shopping for your ring as soon as possible. Do you trust me? Do you love me enough to take this step with me?"

"Yes, TJ, I do love and trust you, but I don't want to force you into getting married."

"You aren't forcing me into anything I don't already want. Baby, I want you to be my wife, to have my babies. I want us to build a life together. How much do you love me?"

"I love you, I-

"Shh, don't tell me. Show me."

"What about Tam?"

"She and Ben can handle their own business, and you and I will handle ours."

Chapter 28

TAMARA

"Tamara, I'm so sorry?" Ben said as he picked up the phone.

"All I want to know is why," I demanded.

"It's nothing more than a lie. I promise you that I haven't been seeing anyone but you."

"What about the pictures and her saying the baby is yours?"

"Tamara, I can explain. But first know, I never meant for any of this to hurt you or hunt us, but the truth is, I dated Stacey long before I met you."

"Wait! But your brother?" I couldn't believe what I was hearing.

"I know, but this was before I knew anything about her being involved with my brother. I broke things off with her when we started dating. As crazy as it sounds, we all found out that she was engaged to him the night of the party. Sure, Ce spoke about her, and my parents met her, but I hadn't, being that Ce didn't live here. So imagine my shock learning that she knew who my brother was and didn't tell me. After going off on her about it, I hadn't heard from her again until she called me two months later to say that she was pregnant. I did tell her not to worry and that I would take care of what was mine if it were mine. And that I needed a DNA test first. When she found out we were engaged, she got upset, flew off the handle, and threatened to tell you if I didn't call off the wedding. So here we are."

Speechless. I couldn't say anything.

"Hello?"

"I'm still here, Ben. All of this is so hard to believe."

"But baby, it's the truth. I would never purposely hurt or cheat on you. I hope you know within your heart that I'm telling the truth. So please don't throw away what we have over a lie."

"I hear what you are saying, but this hurts so much and way too familiar. She sent pictures, Ben, of the two of you together. Who am I supposed to believe?"

"Believe your man. Tamara, did you look at those pictures?"

"Yes." I snapped back.

"Well then, you saw the dates on them, right? We took those pictures about two years ago. One of them was actually taken the early part of last year."

"Last year?"

"Last year." He confirmed.

"Ben, I'm so sorry," I said, crying. "I just didn't know what to think."

"Sweetheart, come home, or better yet, I can come to you."

"I was way too upset to drive, so Erica brought me to her place."

"Say less, I'm on my way." He said and hung up the phone.

***

I was so happy to see Ben. Last night was so special. I had never seen him so vulnerable. We just laid there holding each other. The thought of being apart was too much for either one of us to take. I wanted to talk more about the possibility of him being the father of Stacey's baby, but I will wait until after the wedding. I didn't want to bring the mood down. Love was most definitely in the air late last night. So much so that TJ and Erica were floating on cloud nine. I hated that Ben and I agreed to wait until our honeymoon to make love again. It was hard, but we made it through without any help from our hosts. Clearly, they forgot that there were guests in their home. Well, at least somebody had a good time, even if we couldn't.

Chapter 29

THE WEDDING

We left Erica's house at ten o'clock this morning. The wedding was going to start at five. My bridal party and I went to the salon to be pampered. We had the entire place to ourselves for hair, nails, and make-up. I was glad that they had more than enough staff to service us. After the pandemic, things became a little iffy for many businesses.

We had pictures to take at two. We left the salon at one to head to the church. My mother was really enjoying herself. I loved how she and Mother Harris have bonded. The only thing that I wished they'd stop talking about was when Ben and I were going to have babies. I would like to walk down the aisle first, ladies.

We made it to the church and dressed. Ben and I chose to take all of our wedding pictures first so we could have more time to celebrate our nuptials with our family and friends. After seeing my handsome groom and taking pictures, I had just enough time to relax in my bridal suite.

My nerves were getting the best of me. With a sprite in one hand and crackers in the other, Maria announced a ten-minute warning. Whatever we couldn't do within those ten minutes would have to wait until afterward. I was still very nervous, but at least the crackers and sprite quieted my rumblings.

The music started to play, and everyone walked down the aisle. The only two left now were Mom and I, and she would be the one to give her baby girl away.

"It's almost our turn, sweetie."

"I know, mama."

"Baby, I am so proud of you, and if your father were here, I know he would be too."

"Stop it. You are going to make me cry."

"I love you, Tammie." She told me.

"I love you too, Mom," I said, trying to keep my composure.

"Okay, baby, let's go." She said after kissing my cheek and pulling down my veil.

I was wearing a beautiful ivory cathedral-length veil. It was trimmed in guipure lace. She and I entered the chapel. It was so beautiful. Ben was standing there looking so handsome in his off-white Tom Ford tuxedo. His groomsmen were wearing the same but in gray. They had gray-colored ties, white shirts, and gray shoes. My bridesmaids were wearing Tiffany blue colored dresses in different styles that complemented each personality and figure. They wore silver accessories and matching strappy sandals. Erica was my maid of honor. Her dress was a beautiful strapless satin ball gown in silver. My dress was simply gorgeous. I was wearing a strapless Vera Wang ivory satin corset ball gown with beaded lace appliques. Attached was my chapel-long train. My wedding bouquet was made of white roses, with Tiffany blue satin ribbon laced around the handle.

This, without question, has been the best day of my life. My mother kissed my cheek again before giving me away to Ben. She shed her tears of joy, and now it was Mother Harris's turn. She read 1 Corinthians, Chapter 13. She made me tear up because she cried while reading the passage. As we lit the unity candles, the soloist's song, *The Prayer*, by Donnie McClurkin and Yolanda Adams. We walked back to Papa Harris and faced each other.

We were now ready to exchange our vows, but before we could, Papa Harris had asked, "Should anyone be present know of any reason why this couple should not be joined in holy matrimony? Speak now or forever hold your peace?"

A hush fell over the church while we stood there smiling at one another.

"I know, just cause." She said.

And the next thing I saw was blackness.

STAY TUNED AS THE SAGA CONTINUES...

A Thin Line Between Sex and Lies: Old Flames

COMING IN 2024

How did you like the book?

Share your thoughts with me at ddmiles.author@gmail.com.

Want to Read More

Feel free to visit me on the web at

www.relationshipreflections.org.

Made in the USA
Monee, IL
20 August 2024

63675258R00134